queens of all the earth

Hannah Sternberg

bancroft
press

Published by Bancroft Press
"Books that enlighten"
800-637-7377
P.O. Box 65360, Baltimore, MD 21209
410-764-1967 (fax)
www.bancroftpress.com

Cover Design: Hannah E. Sternberg
Author Photo: Brandon Stewart
Interior Design: Tracy Copes

Hardcover 978-1-61088-019-0
Paperback 978-1-61088-032-9
Library of Congress
Control Number: 2011938093 (HC)
Printed in the United States of America

For Mom,
whose heart is open to little birds

they are

alone

he beckons, she rises she

stands

a moment

in the passion of the fifty

pillars

listening

while the queens of all the

earth writhe upon deep rugs

- E. E. Cummings, "Orientale"

0

IT MAY NOT
ALWAYS BE SO

At Cornell University in upstate New York, a thousand incoming freshmen milled through a dozen entry booths, collecting keys and pamphlets and signing waivers, meeting their roommates, bickering with their parents, then hugging their parents when they hoped their roommates weren't looking.

In Williamsburg, Virginia, a rented van waited, packed tight with the fruits of a shopping spree. Virtually everything inside was new, much of it still in its original packaging. Unflinching summer sunlight made the van's contents appear chintzy, forlorn.

A hastily parked car straddled the grass beside the driveway of the house where the van waited. The front door of the house stood slightly open.

"We know it's not physical," the doctor upstairs told Miranda Somerset. "As the paramedics told you, her vitals are normal. The problem is in the mind."

Dr. Simons was a family friend from the College of William and Mary, where Miranda's mother worked. He was primarily an academic psychologist. At first, Miranda had called 9-1-1, but then she panicked after the paramedics told her they couldn't compel a legal adult to undergo a psychiatric evaluation if she wasn't a threat to herself or others. The paramedics left quietly, with a deflated sense of emergency, but Miranda's anxiety rose. She called her mother, who was giving a paper in Middlebury, for some shred of advice, and her mother had told her to call Dr. Simons.

"Is there something you can give her? Valium or something? Something to get her through it?" Miranda asked Dr. Simons. "Just to get her out of bed? I'm sure as soon as she starts moving, she'll feel better."

"Miranda," he said with the patience of someone used to negotiating with deniers, "she's had a full psychotic break. She isn't going anywhere."

"Move-in ends at 5 p.m.," Miranda said, unaware of the tear rolling down her cheek.

In the bedroom beyond the door where Miranda and Dr. Simons stood, the August sun sluiced through the gap where the blinds didn't drop down all the way, creating a hard bright line on the floor. The mug of coffee Miranda had brought upstairs for her sister sat cold as granite on the nightstand. Olivia lay like a rock on her bed. Her eyes, peeled, stared at the ceiling. Beads of perspiration stood round and perfect on her forehead, though the room was cool.

Her left hand clutched a book from her childhood, *A Swiftly Tilting Planet*, a time-travel adventure. Her index finger held her place between the pages. Miranda had not been able to remove the book from her hands, and Dr. Simons, when he had arrived, had advised against trying.

"She shouldn't be alone," Dr. Simons said, glancing at Olivia.

"I can take another day off work," Miranda said. Miranda, seven years older than her sister, lived in Arlington, Virginia, where she worked as an accountant for an insurance company.

"Good. Talk to her. Play music she likes. Bring her food. Let her smell it," Dr. Simons said. "She's in there somewhere. My guess is she'll come out again sooner rather than later. Call me again tomorrow."

"Are you sure there isn't anything you can give her?"

"There's nothing physically wrong with her," the doctor repeated. "And I can't prescribe anything until she's undergone a full psychological evaluation. I wouldn't want to, even if I could. We don't know what we're dealing with until she decides to open up and start talking about it. Could be major depression, could be bipolar disorder." He took off his glasses and cleaned them on a corner of his jacket. "But considering her history, and your family's history, it's most probably nothing more than brief reactive psychosis. In that case, I'd recommend avoiding medication and letting her rest and recover at her own pace, with the help of therapy."

In the bedroom, Olivia heard but didn't hear the words being said about her. She had heard the Metronomic alarm, steady and faithful like her breathing, but she also hadn't heard it, as if she were buried somewhere deep below the ocean, where all this sound and outside sensation fused into a solid block, a barrier between herself and now.

She had already been awake for an hour when the alarm went off, watching the ceiling grow from a pale shadow to a crisp white constellation of bubbles. Her alarm had wailed for another hour before Miranda had stormed into her room to wake her up.

The shouting. The pleading. The phone calls. The pounding on the stairs. Olivia had heard and not heard them. Her eyes were not glassy, but intense and focused.

"Can't you stay a little longer?" Miranda asked Dr. Simons. "I don't want to be . . ." She didn't finish the sentence. "I'm worried if she gets any worse," she said.

Dr. Simons looked at his watch.

"I can stay another hour or so," he said.

The new freshmen of Cornell University were plugging in their microwaves, discovering which of their desk toys had broken in transit, and comparing video game consoles. Their residence advisors were completing complicated checklists placed on battered clipboards. In another hour, many of the freshmen would disperse to find lunch, hoping they'd be able to find their way back to their rooms again.

Olivia didn't leave her room. She didn't move or speak all that morning. She did not set aside her book or remove her finger from the page it marked.

Dr. Simons sent one of his graduate students to sit by Olivia's bed in the afternoon, while Miranda unloaded the rental van and returned it. Dr. Simons picked Miranda up from the rental facility and took her home. She arrived to the sound of children's playful screams from the inflatable pool next-door.

That evening, as if she'd sensed the specter of the van was gone, Olivia sighed and turned her face to the side.

Dr. Simons and his graduate student went home.

That night, their mother called and asked Miranda to hold the phone to Olivia's ear.

"This is perfectly natural," their mother said. "Most adolescents fear the onset of adulthood. You'll come out of it, honey. In the meantime, let Miranda feed you some supper, okay?"

Olivia's silence was her only response.

That night, the freshmen of Cornell acted as if they were too cool to wish they were at home.

The Somersets' neighbors' children slept, perfectly convinced no day could be as wonderful as today, except tomorrow.

Olivia slept that night, white under the sheets.

1

THEY ARE ALONE

It was November.

It had taken more than three months to lift Olivia out of the fog, to find her voice and shake it out, and then to pry her from the house, not for school, but for what Miranda called an "educational journey" to Spain—a test run, an emotional stability experiment, or, if Miranda squinted, a vacation. A vacation from the last three months.

Olivia was on the bus from the airport to Barcelona. The bus was moving very fast. She felt the bumps and swayed with the turns, languidly reaching for the bar in front of her while her sister clutched the edge of the seat and scowled. Maybe the bus was not moving at all; maybe the scenery was moving very fast. Mountains, green dragon-like and ridge-backed, rippled past with bulges like vertebrae, snaking around the bus and hoarding in their center a softly glowing red and yellow city. Their summits reared and roared and shrank back again, hiding and then revealing small pink houses.

Olivia sat thinking about mountains. She had never seen mountains like this, except in pictures. It was like discovering the monsters on the map were no joke at all.

The spirit of adventure had not filled her yet, not like when she read of it in books. The telephone lines sliced through the scene, and the dance pop on the radio and the dreary desolation of the highway grated at her fantasies until they were shed like flakes of old skin. In reality, travel was sweaty and painful, fraught with baseless fears, minor accidents, and lingering dehydration headaches. She scattered these thoughts into the now-clear (and still smarting) acre of her mind reserved for adventure, where imagination had previously flourished and occasionally grown strange flowers.

That August, Olivia's nervous breakdown had seemed to fade after a few days. Her mother had called it a "catatonic episode," much like some aboriginal mystical experiences undergone at the coming of age. Olivia and Miranda's mother was a sociological anthropology professor of some repute at William and Mary. She traveled often in the summer, conducting research and conferring with other tireless scholars. She had cleared her schedule as soon as she had come home, however, allowing Miranda to return to her own job and home in Arlington.

In the space of three days, Olivia had emerged from her dream state, wandering her room and touching familiar things. Then she had begun obediently to come down for breakfast, lunch, and dinner, never preparing anything for herself but instead waiting patiently at the table, even if it took her mother, elsewhere in the house, hours to realize she was there. She had even begun to speak.

That was how Miranda, visiting the next weekend to check on her sister, had realized that the episode was not over yet.

On the bus to Barcelona, Miranda sighed. She wished the driver would slow down.

As her sister, next to her, reached for the bar in front of them, Miranda clutched the edge of her seat. She had insisted they sit up front to see the city as they approached, but now, as she watched the road with the vigilance the driver should have had, she tapped her foot on an imaginary brake. Travel was difficult, she knew from experience, and the only way to shake total exhaustion was activity, activity, activity.

When they arrived, they would begin sightseeing immediately. They would take a few pictures on Miranda's new digital camera to send to their mother to prove to her they had arrived. They would eat a meal at dinnertime and remain awake until 10 p.m. local time. This Sunday would be a prizefight between herself and sleep, and she would pound exhaustion to pieces, even if that meant ending up black and blue herself.

Miranda moved very fast in the bus to Barcelona. The numbing desire to lie down and do nothing crept up to her eyeballs. She suppressed it and prepared herself to take up the fight for her sister.

She watched the road.

Together they tumbled with the bus, through ridge-backed dragon-green mountains, past the pink houses that bobbed into and out of sight like shards of spectrums in a spinning prism.

"I don't want to go."

"Miranda's already called in and explained the situation. They're letting you defer your first semester."

"No, Mom. I don't want to go."

"You can take the whole year if that's what you need. The important thing is that you get better."

Silence.

"Don't you want to get better, honey? Don't you want to be with people your age again?"

Huff. "You don't get it."

"I think I understand quite clearly what's going on here." Sharply.

"If I go," slowly, deliberately, "the kids next-door will disappear."

Pained sigh. "Honey, you know that's not true. You can't really believe that."

"If I go, they'll be stolen and replaced. There are things in the night that do that." Matter-of-fact.

Getting up. "How about this. You can stay as long as you need to, but in return you have to go see Dr. Simons twice a week. Deal?"

"He doesn't get it. He'll just tell me I'm making it all up."

"Okay, new deal. You go, or I take all your books away and give them to charity."

"Mom, you can't do that!"

"You've outgrown them all anyway. I can see now I shouldn't have let you keep rereading them like that."

"No you can't take my books they're special they're the only thing that can save those kids Mom no you can't do it please Mom no don't do it it'll kill them—"

"Shh, shh, I won't, I won't, I promise I won't. You just have to go see Dr. Simons."

Dr. Simons had said Olivia needed "closure." The word "closure" had a great deal of power over them all.

Lack of closure, Dr. Simons said, was what prevented Olivia from letting go of her childhood. It was the reason she had made only a few scattered friends in high school. It was behind her silence and then, later, behind her delusions.

Dr. Simons talked to Olivia about her father, who had left them long before she could remember him, and had died with equal invisibility earlier that summer. His disappearance had been so thorough that when Miranda declined to attend the funeral, Olivia wondered if they had both mentally buried him long before.

The doctor talked to her about her sexual history, which was utterly blank and calm. He talked to her about her mother. He talked to her about her sister. He talked to her about the children next-door. She had a bright, strong, healthy mind that gradually let go of its delusions like a flower letting go of its petals at the end of summer.

The blue period followed fantasy.

Dr. Simons encouraged her to garden. Her mother agreed. Contact with nature, she said, was traditionally believed to improve the mood and mental functions of depression sufferers. Their mother used the word "depression" clinically, as if she was ripping off a Band-Aid to show Olivia exactly where it hurt, and Olivia felt her eye twitch every time she heard it. She had recovered just enough feeling to be humiliated by the past month, which plunged her deeper into that dark place inside her that had opened up at the thought of leaving home.

But as the autumn grayed, so did the soothing effect of being home. Losing its leaves and scratching at the ease of mind Olivia so desperately strove to cultivate, autumn at home left her raw and terrified again. With tedious melancholy, home turned on her. Miranda saw it too, and saw the opportunity to promote her own route to closure: travel.

Their mother didn't believe in Thanksgiving, so Miranda, who had the week off, suggested a vacation to Barcelona. Miranda had spent a semester in Spain when she was in college, and she hoped the experience would lift her sister out of her torpor and make her feel readier for Cornell. Their mother wasn't coming—she had to be at Dartmouth to interview a published expert on the influence of Orientalism on existentialists in front of a panel of interdisciplinary literary critics and social scientists.

Olivia and Miranda blew out of their childhood home along with the last leaves of autumn, then tumbled from car to plane to bus, and finally to the streets of Barcelona.

Olivia, outside herself, watched the scenes of her first European city bob past like washed-out hand-held film footage as she and Miranda made their way on foot from the bus stop to the hostel. In the corner of an abandoned store window sat a sign faded by the sun, its letters obscured except for one surviving question mark.

The scent of sewage and things frying sent bullets into Olivia's already pounding head, and on La Rambla, the artery of Barcelona with the broad, shady promenade down its center, each heavy impact of her puffy feet on the wide, sunny pavement echoed in the tender portions of her skull. It was bright, and she was tired; her hands and arms were cramped and her mouth was sticky, and she consistently patted each of her pockets to affirm their custody of important contents, followed occasionally by a nervous crane over her shoulder to glance at the zipper on her backpack.

Mostly, she looked at her feet, trying not to step on the trash that was foreign only in being printed in another language, while bearing the logos she knew well. When she looked up, she could only squint, and so her first glimpses of Barcelona were painful, brief slices of pedestrian signals and street signs.

They arrived at the address Miranda had written down. An exiting couple let them in without question through the creaking iron and glass street door of Sixty-Four La Rambla. Olivia rushed in with evident relief, but Miranda lingered a moment in the doorway to scowl at this breach of security.

Then Miranda, with a confidence that Olivia had not yet learned to question, led them across the tiled and barely lit foyer and into the twilight of the narrow marble staircase that slithered up the center of the building, encircling a cage elevator. The Casa Joven was on the third floor of a relatively plain and forgotten Art-Nouveau building that bisected the edges of the city's medieval and nineteenth-century districts.

Below the hostel, a notary and an architect lurked behind elaborately carved wooden doors set with stained glass, defying the shabby decay of the narrow stair they opened onto. Olivia paused for a nanosecond when she thought she saw a question mark faintly chalked in the dim grime of the stairwell wall, but Miranda pulled her past it before she could get a good look.

The Casa Joven, like the businesses below it, was hidden behind a square, hulking green door with a brass knob protruding from the exact center, a door that hung ajar, and Olivia, rising toward it, had a sense that if only it had opened an inch wider, she would have had a glimpse of fantastically intimate scenes of life unfolding just around its edge.

But instead, when Miranda pushed it open, she saw only a narrow passage, cubby-holing a computer, and a sour-faced, blond receptionist. Olivia crowded in awkwardly behind Miranda, jostling both her and the little reception desk as she tried to find a way to get her backpack out of the path of the closing door. After an agonizing moment, she emerged on the right side of the entry hall, leaving her sister to confirm their booking as if she were twelve and Miranda was her mother. Her bags had grown heavier the closer they'd approached their goal, and Olivia now dropped them on the floor of the common room with a wracking groan.

"We have reservations," she heard Miranda say as she looked around.

Feeling the weight of weary muscles finally relieved, Olivia drank in the safety of stillness, letting the room enclose her and protect her from the painful and strange outside. She looked around the common room, letting her eyes wander from the couches slouching against the left wall, hugging the parquet floor, to the island of the faded braid rug, to the opposite wall harboring two dining tables and a fleet of spindly chairs. Turning to look behind her, she took in the kitchen in a nook open to the rest of the room, beside the mouth of the hall with the reception computer.

At the back of the common room, a wooden arch supported by lotus-shaped columns embellished a single step up, beyond which a sunken recliner hid in the corner and three computers clustered in front of a large bare window. Olivia took a step toward the window when the recliner moved. It had grown a hand; there was a person inside it.

He leaned forward and materialized as an adolescent about her age, his gangly height folded around a book. His eyes, which seemed to speak when he didn't, met hers, and then he looked up at the ceiling above her head. Her glance followed his. Above her, strands of a sunburst shot from the center of the hanging lamp.

It was then the room became whole, crystallizing from assorted elements into a hard and definite shape: the painting on the ceiling, geometric and bright with visible brushstrokes; the angular details of the wooden arch, notched by collisions; the footpaths worn into the braided rug.

Then her sister touched her elbow and it all evaporated into invisible ordinariness again, and the silent reader in the chair made himself invisible, too, having turned the beacon of his eyes back to his book.

They followed the blond girl through the right of the common room into a short corridor with doors on both sides and a bathroom at the end.

"On the left, at the back," the blond girl said, and with a flash of keys into Miranda's hand, she abandoned the sisters in the corridor.

Miranda and Olivia opened the left door into a long room, where paired bunk beds multiplied in neat rows toward the small window at the back, providing enough sleeping space for about ten people. At the very end was a bunk wedged against the window, which Olivia assumed was "the back." She shuffled toward it with their things while Miranda followed with hesitation, looking critically around the room.

"Wait, is this *our* room?" Miranda called out the door. "This isn't *our* room, is it?" But the blond girl was nowhere to be seen.

With numb absence of mind, Olivia scrutinized the flower-specked cotton duvet rolled at the end of a neighboring bunk.

"This can't possibly be our room," Miranda said, her confusion growing into anger.

Olivia looked up.

"Where is she? This *can't* be our room," Miranda said again, more sharply.

"What's wrong with it?" Olivia asked.

"I could have sworn I booked a room for two."

"Yeah, well, we get the whole bunk, both the beds—"

"No, like a private room for two. I *know* I booked a private room for two. I've got it on our reservation."

"Maybe the other beds aren't filled," Olivia said, sitting on the empty one she had been examining as if to make her point.

"No, there's a suitcase under that bunk. And," Miranda said, advancing toward the door and between two bunks, "there are boxer shorts over here."

"Miranda, those were under someone's pillow!"

"Oh my God, they put us in a mixed dorm!"

"I'm sure it's just a misunderstanding."

"Don't they have computers to keep things straight? I can't believe I trusted the reviewers from Australia."

Olivia could not think of a defense for the Australian reviewers, so instead, she took off her shoes and asked, "Top or bottom?"

"Oh, it's up to you," Miranda said, disgorging her purse onto the bottom bunk. "You know I'm afraid of heights."

Olivia creaked up to the top bunk and the bed squealed.

"Would you just listen to that?" Miranda continued, finding her pace and sticking to it. "I can't even see any support for it under here. The top one's just resting on a bracket. I bet it would fall down any minute and crush someone in their sleep."

"Do you want me to take the bottom bunk?" Olivia asked.

"No, just don't wiggle too much. Anyway, don't get comfortable. I'm going to find that blond girl and get this all sorted out. Hopefully we can change today before we unpack." Miranda sneezed. "I think I'm allergic to something in here. Probably the wool blankets. And the dust."

With her hands under her head, Olivia quietly (and gently) stretched out under her wool blanket. The ceiling, she noted, was stained rich gold where sunlight spilled in through the window by her bed and faded to cool blue in the darker depths of the room.

"I'll be right back," Miranda said. "And don't fall asleep! If you sleep in the middle of the day, you'll never kill the jet lag."

Olivia listened to Miranda march down the corridor and heard the opening volley of a heated encounter between people who knew only maybe five words in common, though she was moderately confused because one of the voices was male. Olivia felt an accustomed discomfort at the discharge of her sister's outrage, but it couldn't pique her for long in her exhaustion. With passive defiance, she let sleep steal over her. Miranda could command her to stay awake but would never wake her once she was peacefully dozing.

It was then she became aware of how precarious her bed was, because it was floating, floating.

She dreamed of home, where trees with rain-darkened bark, bare and lace-like, scratched at the sky, and the scents of cider and wood smoke slithered around and into her with warm familiarity. She dreamed of her mother hugging her goodbye, and the scratch of her mother's knitted sweater against her cheek, and the wool blankets they kept in the closet for sitting on when the grass was damp. She did not see the ceiling close to her nose, but the wallpaper in her own bedroom, and the table upon which her lamp sat, and her red-glowing alarm clock.

But even in her dream, her old bedside lamp became the rail of the hostel bunk bed; her alarm clock, the glow of the sun through faded orange curtains. Her blanket didn't smell like home, but like strangers. The familiar things spun from her one by one, as her sleeping mind struggled with the notion that they weren't just around the corner. She was jerked awake by the sudden fear that she was falling back into the darkness where she had been before. The doctor had said it was possible.

She was surrounded by a crowd of terrors. She couldn't remember where she was, or what time it was, or *who* she was, only that she was floating somewhere in the midst of alien sensations. Her limbs had acquired the stiffness of travel and deep sleep, and briefly she imagined herself paralyzed, though eventually she understood it was only heavy lethargy between spans of unconsciousness. She could, however, exert herself enough to look, through clouded eyes and with shallow breath, at the commotion around her.

A girl was bending over the bed a few rows down, the one distinguished by its hidden boxer shorts, and from a nearby corner a man hummed to himself. The silhouettes of two more male figures haunted the farthest end of the room. The murmuring double pillars of their bodies were solid. With a wave of new energy, she sat up toward them, but as she did so, a door between them closed and their voices and forms were trapped on the other side.

The other voices remained, and gradually, Olivia, tilting her head from one side to the other and squinting, worked out that the other two men had been in the other room on the opposite side of the alcove. She watched with unnatural stillness as a pair of girls and the humming man bustled out of the dormitory; she saw lights in the corridor appear and disappear and heard water and toilets running and music somewhere and unintelligible conversation.

By the time complete awareness of her own body returned, with tingling sensations down her toes and the stab of an angry muscle in her shoulder, the room had expelled the rest of its living contents, leaving only Olivia and the sound of Miranda's soft snoring. A green glowing clock beside another traveler's bed told her it was seven in the evening— dinnertime. Of course, Olivia reflected, Miranda could contradict her own edict, but Olivia was too exhausted to resent her for long, and resentment wasn't a natural reaction for her anyway.

The door was shut at last by a considerate hand on the outside, and the sisters were again in darkness, except for the dim glow of streetlights from the window by their bunk. Olivia rolled toward the window, pushed the curtain aside, and looked out. Below was a stamp-sized garden framed by successive rooftop balconies and terraces that contributed green tendrils to its miniature wilderness. From the railings of the building opposite, a few sheets and towels fluttered against pale patches of interior light.

It was rustic and charming enough that Olivia could imagine the place as a scene in a book, safe and comfortable and fictional. The day's sensations had overwhelmed her with a cacophonous mess of the alien and the familiar: rows of trendy fashion shops swelling the lower levels of intricate Iberian homes; a KFC leering over the corner down the block, across from a tapas bar with its front walls folded away and open to the street like a Parisian café.

Olivia had never been so homesick in her entire life. The prospect of a week surrounded by strangers filled her with dull dread.

Safe in her position above stray eyes, Olivia had a thorough, quiet cry over the dejection of a long day of stressful travel. The shaking and possibly the effort of cleansing herself of that sticky unhappiness finished for her the work of waking.

A gnawing hunger pulled on her nerves, and she tentatively stole down the ladder. Miranda, in her sleeping mask and earplugs, would never know.

In the twilight and the chill, slightly autumnal air, the dormitory felt suspended, a bubble in antique glass, somewhere between home and Barcelona. Olivia touched the bunks as she passed, the sting of cool metal grounding her. She swam through the evening atmosphere to the door and, with a creak, peered out. Here were the sounds of life again, warm brightness, and the scent of food. Gathering courage, she slipped out at last and pattered toward them.

In the common room, a Spanish pop station played cheery dance beats under the susurrus of a dozen people attempting to converse in at least four languages—Romantic, Germanic, and some that were neither, or so heavily accented they sounded only like a jumble of meaningless sounds. Among one group, the prevalent color seemed to be a bold shade of blue, displayed on shirts and scarves and even in the pattern of a kilt. Elsewhere, a cluster of twenty-somethings in stylishly decomposed layers of tank-tops and uselessly thin sweaters lobbed vague recommendations at each other.

A man in his thirties spoke more quietly to two familiar shapes, who had first appeared to Olivia as dark pillars but now revealed themselves as the reader from the corner and an older man, visibly related. Dancing around the edges and into the middle of it all, and then out again, was one young woman who seemed to be trying to speak to everyone at once.

The smell that had pulled her toward this confusion, she identified as a combination of omelets, spaghetti, and stir-fried green vegetables. As a meal, the collection was about as organized and sensible as the words coming from the mouths of the combined crowd.

The light fell on Olivia and soon she was seen.

A young man in a black staff shirt greeted her, in Spanish, with an infectious smirk. She didn't understand much of what he said, except she thought she caught Miranda's name. Something about his broad smile assured Olivia of its permanence, but at the same time made her feel special, as if its warmth was extended to her most of all. However, he quickly turned with equal nonchalance and directed his attention to brighter objects.

Looking past the staffer, Olivia inadvertently met the tall reader's eyes again, and recognition ignited his. Olivia, with a burning feeling, realized she was once again standing directly below the sunburst.

The boy stepped toward her. He smiled in a quiet, sad way, with his mouth closed.

"Do you want anything?" he asked, shrugging toward the tables scattered with food.

"I—um," she began and stopped, surprised at how hoarse her voice was. The boy's relative looked over and joined them before she could find another word.

"Why, hello there," the older one said cheerily. He was barely her height, a soft, gray-haired man with a round face and young eyes. "You must be Miranda's sister," he said. She found her hand being grasped warmly by both of his, and then released. "Now, now," he said, taking something out of his pocket and shaking it out. It was a handkerchief. "Such a pretty face," he said in a soft Southern burr, patting her cheeks with the worn cloth. "Now why's it all wet?"

She wished she knew. Olivia sniffed. She hadn't noticed that her eyes were still welling. She wished she could sink into the floor. The older man just smiled gently.

"Let Greg get you something," he said. "You just sit yourself down."

Olivia couldn't. She was already embarrassed by her tears and certain she was be the least interesting, least traveled person in the room. And apparently, they all knew about Miranda's tirade.

Olivia shook her head and, without any further response, turned and slipped out of the room. She returned, shivering, to the calm, smothering darkness of the dorm room and, mesmerized by the sound of Miranda's whispery snoring, waited with unnatural stillness for the other sleepers to return.

2

THIS MOTIONLESS FORGETFUL WHERE

Olivia refused to leave the dorm room by herself the next morning. That way she wouldn't have to worry about overhearing people talk about her sister. So she and Miranda washed their faces together, rubbing the sleep-crumbs from their eyes over the same mirror. The sisters entered the chilly common room swathed in sweatshirts, with their morning hair hand-combed clumsily, their faces a matching set: big spoon and little spoon.

The young guy with the black staff shirt and the welcoming smile wandered in and out of the common room with a pail and a mop, but the two objects never seemed to meet each other or any horizontal surface. The waspish blond girl in braids who had welcomed them when they first arrived was engrossed by one of the computers at the back of the room—was she avoiding Miranda? Two unshaven, ashen-faced men leaned lazily against the lotus columns near her, smoking their morning cigarettes. The other three travelers in the room ate a traditional breakfast at the tables against the wall.

Olivia recognized once again the reader from yesterday and his older relative at the far table, so it was a relief that Miranda steered her toward the emptier table, where a lone woman—the talkative one from last night—buttered her toast. She looked mid-twenties, about Miranda's age, her short straight hair gathered in a spiky ponytail at the back of her head. She had the defiant ease of a person who wasn't waiting for anyone. They sat across from her.

"I didn't know breakfast was included," Miranda whispered to Olivia, ineffectively attempting to maintain the privacy of their conversation. "I guess it makes up for things a little."

"What's wrong?" the other woman at the table asked in a jarring American accent. "If you need another pillow, ask Hugo. He brought me four last night when I asked for one, and I think one of them was his." She smirked.

"I specifically booked a private room for two," Miranda said, "and they stuck us in the mixed dorm. And when I talked to Hugo about it yesterday, he pretended he didn't speak English, which I know can't be true."

Olivia wondered briefly if Miranda realized that, were she correct, Hugo, nearby with his mop, would overhear her quite clearly. Someone else did.

"I have a private room," the older man at the next table called over with no embarrassment. "My son Greg and I are sharing it."

Miranda smiled tightly.

"That's nice."

Their tablemate leaned forward and, her back to the two men, whispered (far more effectively than Miranda), "Those are the Browns. Beware. I try to ignore them, but they can't catch a hint. Either of them. It's like it's genetic."

"Why?"

"The dad's a Baptist minister or something. Kinda creepy, kinda *off*, socially. From the South, sorta crazy, you know, like the spirit catches them and they fall down, or whatever." She leaned back. "Hey, I don't think I caught your names. I'm Lenny Hawkins."

Lenny ventured a hand, which was grasped with restrained enthusiasm.

"Real name's Eleanor, but I hate it," Lenny said. "It's such an old-person name." She laughed.

Miranda's response was a prolonged blink, but Olivia could tell her sister was thawing.

"We're from the South too, actually. Virginia," Miranda said after their names. "Our mom moved down from New England, but our dad is—was—from a real old Southern family. The library is named after them—the Somerset Public Library."

"I can't imagine being settled in a place that long. Grew up a military brat, and I've had itchy feet since I was a kid," Lenny said. "I've lived in Berlin, Dublin, Edinburgh, Johannesburg. Spent some time in New Delhi. My favorite so far is Hong Kong, though. I'm telling you, the future is Asia. Go east, young woman. There's a great breakfast bar there run by an Aussie. Best eggs I've had in my life, and the menu is in Cantonese."

"Didn't you worry about the bird flu?"

"This guy kept his own chickens, on the roof. I'm surprised they didn't get altitude sickness. He was a real crazy."

While Miranda interrogated Lenny about Barcelona, Olivia watched as Mr. Brown caught Hugo on his second pass from back bathroom to hall. They spoke—Olivia couldn't tell in what language—and Mr. Brown beckoned his son, who followed the pair down and away into the hall that led to the far side of the hostel, to the dark unmapped region of the manager's rooms.

"We thought we'd do Gaudí today," Miranda was saying. She was talking about Barcelona's most famous architect. "But we don't want to go all the way out to the park. That kills practically half a day, and it's just one thing."

"I can do Gaudí in half a day, tops. Why don't I show you later this week?" Lenny said. "No park, but we can hit up all the other major stuff."

"What are you doing this morning?" Miranda asked.

"There's a walking tour of the Gothic Quarter," Lenny replied. The Gothic Quarter, or *Barri Gótic*, was the central and oldest part of Barcelona, where many of the original medieval buildings stood intact, framing narrow winding streets tangled like a heap of yarn. "If you're ready in ten minutes, you can tag along. It's a great way to get to know Barcelona— walk from the middle ages to the nineteenth century in a day. And it's free, which is freakin' awesome."

"How about it, Olivia?" Miranda said.

Olivia was fine with it. She was fine with not waiting for the toast. She was fine with putting off writing her e-mail home. As Lenny left the table to get ready, Miranda probed each concern, checking them off a mental list, finally satisfying herself that if Olivia wasn't thrilled about the trip yet, she was at least resigned.

Just then, without introduction or invitation, the elder Mr. Brown stepped up to the table and said, "Young ladies, we took the liberty of switching rooms with you. Hugo's getting clean sheets, and Greg is moving our things now."

Miranda's mouth dropped open.

"That's very—I couldn't imagine—obviously we couldn't make you move out of your room," she said. She remembered Lenny's warning about the Browns and wondered what the real price of the room was—morning prayer meeting? Spontaneous baptism? Or just a low simmer of kinder-than-thou guilting? Miranda and Olivia hadn't grown up with any religion, and while she hadn't been taught aggressive atheism either, Miranda felt slightly uncomfortable around anyone who professed faith. She wondered whether Mr. Brown was really nice, or just strange.

"You don't have to make us. It's already done," said Mr. Brown.

"That's very—thoughtful—but really . . . I'm sorry, we don't even know you," Miranda said.

"I'm Emery Brown," he said with a gentle smile, as if it resolved the whole matter. It made Miranda boil. "And that's my son, Greg," he continued, indicating the young man who had just passed through, rolling a suitcase with one hand and clutching a mass of pajamas and towels in the other.

Olivia looked down, and Miranda assumed she was embarrassed, too. But then, the private room *would* be best for Olivia. She was still fragile, after all.

"Well, okay, I can pay you the difference," Miranda said, more pertly this time. "Olivia can get our things. I'll go to the ATM and get the cash. We don't want to hold you up after you've been so . . . nice. Let me take care of it right now."

"I thought you wanted to go on the walking tour," Olivia said.

"We'll have to miss it. Unless we can take care of everything fast," Miranda replied. She threw the move onto her growing pile of grievances— the Browns' "good deed" was costing her precious sightseeing time.

"It's only our bags—"

"I'll ask Hugo how much more the Browns' room is, then I can withdraw the money at that bank down the road and bring it back for Mr. Brown," Miranda continued without pausing.

"Well, do what you want, but I'm heading out now," Lenny said, breezing by the confused Mr. Brown without a glance, dropping a small notebook into a nylon backpack as she made her way to the hostel door.

"Oh, could you wait a sec, Lenny? I do really want to go," Miranda said, heaving a sigh.

"I can stay and sort it out," Olivia said, taking them both aback. "I wanted some quiet time this morning anyway."

"Really? Are you sure?" Miranda asked, immediately feeling guilty.

This discomfort, too, was the Browns' fault. "I thought you really wanted to see the Gothic Quarter," she said. "You should let me worry about this stuff."

"It's okay, I'll take a walk by myself."

"No! Mom would never let you!" Their mother would probably never find out, but Miranda still couldn't drop the fear that Olivia could slip into another one of her episodes at any time.

"She can wander with us today if she wants," Mr. Brown said. "Or she can just go with you. We really don't need the money right now—"

"Of course we wouldn't inconvenience you," Miranda said. "And Olivia wouldn't want to intrude on your plans."

"I'm really okay by myself. I'll stick to La Rambla, and I won't go far," Olivia said.

Miranda eyed her, weighing her anxieties against each other. Yes, she could count on Olivia not to stray. It was one thing Olivia had proven she knew how to do very well. "Okay," Miranda said, giving Olivia a quick peck on the cheek and dashing back to the dorm to throw on her jeans.

"You're always welcome to join us," Mr. Brown said to Olivia softly. Over his shoulder, Olivia saw Greg dragging a large, old-fashioned suitcase with no wheels across the hall. Mr. Brown followed her eyes. "Greg!" he called. "Don't do that by yourself—let me help you . . ." Mr. Brown and his son soon disappeared into the dorm room.

Miranda returned with her jacket tied around her shoulders. She noted Mr. Brown's absence with a hint of triumphant relief. "We don't have to tell Mom. I know you like your alone time," she said.

"Have fun," said Olivia.

They were gone before Olivia realized Miranda, in her hurry to collect her jacket and keys and camera and all her little necessary items, hadn't left the bank card behind.

Mr. Brown emerged, Greg following like a gangling shadow, to find

Olivia slumped in a kitchen chair, looking vaguely traumatized.

"Miranda forgot to give me the card," she blurted, as if expecting to head off an accusation. "Um, I think I have a few euro in my purse. I'm so sorry. You've been so nice to us."

"It's nothing," Mr. Brown said, a laugh rounding out his voice. "Don't worry your pretty head. Come with us this morning if you want. We don't have a tour, but I've always thought the best guide is never as good as getting lost."

"Thank you," Olivia said. "I'm still a bit jetlagged, though. I think I'll just wait for Miranda to get back."

Actually, getting lost sounded enormously appealing, but the only thing that frightened Olivia more than the strangers outside was the thought of being trapped in a morning of awkward socialization with a family she'd just met.

Mr. Brown seemed genuinely disappointed, but he didn't press his offer, and he and Greg, who had hung just behind his father, silent and alternately contemplating the floor and the blank middle distance throughout the exchange, soon disappeared through the big green door.

Hugo smiled from the kitchen, mop leaning against the counter, a mug of coffee in his hand. Olivia wondered just how much English he did understand.

Olivia entered the dormitory room for the last time to collect their bags and saw the Browns' things set neatly at the foot of her old bunk. The only other inhabitant of the room was a man sitting up in his bed, writing in a small black notebook.

"I see we're losing you for the Browns," he said good-naturedly. "I hope you enjoy your new room."

"Thanks, I'm sure we will," she said. Then, sitting down suddenly, despite the fact that it was no longer her bed, she asked, "Do you know much about them?"

"The Browns? Are they the Mormons?" He had a soft accent—Spanish? South American?—that made what he said sound interesting. "Either way, good people," he said.

"Lenny doesn't seem to be a fan."

"Lenny is the sort of person who will decide whether she likes someone depending on how cleverly she can praise or abuse them."

"*You* don't like Lenny."

"I don't dislike Lenny."

They both smiled, and the nervousness melted away.

"I'm Olivia. I'm here with my sister, Miranda," said Olivia.

"Marc Castillo," he said. "I'm taking holy orders in Lima next year, but I'm traveling first."

"Nice to meet you," Olivia said, and she meant it.

"You can still meet everyone while you're here," he said, "even though you don't get to see them naked anymore."

Olivia laughed.

"I think I've seen most of them by now," she said. "But two of the beds I thought I saw girls in last night are empty."

"People come and go pretty frequently," Marc said. "But as far as I know, there are a number of us staying the whole week. The Browns, I think—they arrived the same day as me, the day before yesterday—and there are two Scottish men here for the football who made it a holiday."

"Are they the ones in the blue jerseys?" Olivia asked.

"Yes indeed," Marc replied.

"I thought I heard them talking in another language."

"No, they're just Scottish."

Olivia smiled. "How long are you here?"

"I stay until Saturday."

Olivia was relieved to hear that like her and her sister, at least one other guest was staying all week. She'd have a chance to get used to at least one of their fellow travelers. There was even a slight possibility she'd stop feeling awkward around him by the end of the week.

As she packed and repacked a pair of socks, Olivia asked, "What are you doing this morning?"

"I'm attending a history lecture reserved for visiting clergy in the cultural institute," said Marc. "Otherwise, I wouldn't mind—"

"That's okay. I hope your lecture is fun."

Olivia had little trouble moving their bags into the new room, which, though not spacious, was surprisingly comfortable. She sat at the small window looking out, mesmerized by the clicking sound of the rotating fan in the corner that, oddly, constructed a conscious silence in the room. She thought of the Browns, their unfaltering kindness contrasted with Miranda's pointless nastiness. But worse, she caught herself wondering which bed had been Greg's, running her hand over the pillow.

Overcome by wilting embarrassment, she escaped to the common room with her novel.

Olivia had brought with her *A Wrinkle in Time*. She had always liked to reread her favorite books, and even after her delusions receded, she was still comforted by the fantasy novels she had read as a child: *The Hobbit*, *A Wrinkle in Time*, *Silver on the Tree*. Now each page carried the memory of another time she had read it, and the images of the fantastic worlds they described were intertwined with pictures of the maple tree at home, the smell of its fallen leaves piled so high she could make a little fort of them and crawl inside—or was she just that small? Sometimes she was shocked to come across the places in her house where she used to hide, only to realize how big she had become. When she read her childhood books, it was as if she shrank so small that no responsibilities and demands could ever find her—she became so small that she disappeared.

But today, the common room kept distracting her. The lotus stalks that held up the alcove's arch seemed to turn real and fertile and green, part of the living architecture of the world. The room wouldn't stay a room.

I'll go read outside, she told herself. The goal of finding a place to alight and read would keep her from going too far, the book would be a shield against unwanted attention, and the open space would relieve her of the feeling that the room was watching her.

Determined that nothing, not even herself, would stop her, she left the Casa Joven with keys in her pocket and book clutched to her side, as if it is a talisman. Without a map, and probably not nearly enough extra layers of clothing to make her mother or Miranda happy, she looked for the ghostly question mark she'd thought she'd seen in the stairwell yesterday, but it had been rubbed out, if it had ever been there to begin with. The green door swung open for her, and the marble steps tipped her down gently to the street, where she set out into brilliant sunshine.

3

NOWHERE TO HERE,
NEVER TO BEAUTIFUL

The beginning of Olivia's adventure was not auspicious. The same week she and her sister were visiting Barcelona, a soccer match had drawn half the population of Scotland to the city, so that wherever she turned, she felt surrounded by inebriated men in blue kilts.

Other touches of the bizarre here in the Gothic Quarter more appealed to Olivia's romantic imagination. Street stalls housed terrified gerbils, rabbits, and guinea pigs, crowded into the empty cages meant to carry them to their eventual homes. In the backs of stalls, canaries, parrots, and pigeons (whether domesticated or simply caught in the park, Olivia couldn't guess) vied vociferously for attention. In another memorable stall, turkeys, chickens, and a rooster called out in their distinct languages. The street-wise pigeons that landed atop their cages seemed to deliver messages from the outside world, and they were all probably well informed about how many people were swimming that day and where the traffic was bad.

And over the whole scene, the November sun washed warm and

warming, and embodied a new color Olivia had never sampled before. It made the ancient buildings swell and breathe, and the carved waterspouts of goblins and saints stretch strenuously into the air, as if to tear themselves away and fly above the caged canaries and spilled beer of La Rambla. The side streets became narrower, taller, and darker, taking mysterious curves to unknown places, and Olivia, overcome with a brightness not quite happiness but close to the sensation of living, veered into one at random.

It was darker in the alley, though no less crowded, and while the arm of tourist commerce still stretched into the seedy storefronts there, the wares became more interesting and creative. Scarves and shoes that looked suspiciously second-hand piled up along the sides of store alcoves that opened directly onto the street. There was a mask shop, dark and inviting with a carved sign. Her book forgotten, Olivia descended into the store, brain full of phantom masquerades, hidden daggers, and stolen jewels.

Some masks had pointed beaks, and others were covered in scales and had bright feathers that formed ridges and spikes along the sleek lines of their silhouettes, like the mountains she had driven over yesterday. The little shop smelled of papier-mâché and old wood. Olivia ran her fingers over an eye mask covered in sheet music and wondered what it would sound like if played exactly as it appeared. She bought it.

Somewhere, bells tolled, and they were answered by more bells somewhere else, hidden between the folds of the rippling orange-colored city. Olivia heard a music box playing nearby and almost left her mask at the counter of a coffee stall. She drifted without sense or destination until the bells tolled again. Then she saw the spire from which the sound came and walked toward it.

But walking in a straight line in the Gothic Quarter of Barcelona was nearly impossible, and while the latticed and jagged spire hooked her eye and pulled her toward it, it never seemed to grow closer, and she was continually turning, trying to reach it. The stone pavement under her feet was smooth, forgiving, and cool, and led her into a small courtyard. There, past a trail of dark cafés and an obscure hostel with a yellow box sign, businesspeople sat by a fountain eating lunch.

The courtyard was an indefinable geometric shape, the meeting of several strands of alley and the awkward corners of buildings. On her left, the huge castellated wall of the Cathedral (or maybe not the Cathedral but something else that had grown from it) towered like a fat, sleeping beast of mud-colored stone. She had seen pictures of the Cathedral of Barcelona everywhere, from posters in the airport to banners on tour buses. It was so iconic she recognized it even in fragmented slices, but seeing the pictures become real was unexpectedly eerie, like seeing the characters of a movie walk off the screen and into the theater.

From the opposite corner, tucked away in a porch, came music. An accordion and its player spun fugues and requiems, which drifted from that fountainhead into the soft whispering of the street. Olivia couldn't be sure if it was the accordion that breathed in air and exhaled melody, or the palm trees in the portico and the fountain at its center, or the spice- and sewer-scented air that slithered through the arches that contained it all.

As she watched the accordion player, the bells tolled again, joining his song and clashing with it. Drawn to the source of those sounds, Olivia wound her way through the next alley. She thought she saw a question mark faintly chalked on the side of a building, like the one she had glimpsed in the stairwell of the hostel yesterday, but her feet carried her away from it before she could be certain. The bells were very close now, and Olivia followed the current of music, trailing her hand along the side of the castle-like monster, seeking its head. As she followed its flank, the alley widened and the sun poured in. She lost the sound of the accordion player to traffic.

Then she was on the street, and the wall had dropped away into an enclosed dirt square. The spire was just ahead of her. She rounded the corner and at last saw it all, complete and drenched in gold.

From a collection of coy glimpses, it had transformed into a cathedral, spinning toward the sky. It was huge and delicate, so infinitely detailed it made her eyes hurt, and its many small points of beauty jostled for attention until she couldn't comprehend any of them at all and could only stand, looking up. The Cathedral's voice had boomed, and out of respect, the other buildings had receded and formed a square.

If the Cathedral seemed grand and wise, Olivia felt small and ignorant. Her awe turned against her, and she grew frustrated at herself for not being able to recall the facts or trivia about this church that she had read in the books and on the posters and pamphlets that had made it seem so familiar. Even so, she knew what she had read had no relation to what it felt like to stand under the spires shredding the sky.

Shyly, she stepped toward the door.

Three beggars with scarves on their heads sat on the steps, clutching pictures of children.

"*Señorita*, please, I will pray for you."

"Por favor, por los niños."

"Please have pity, *señorita*."

Olivia walked past them as quickly as possible and tried not to look, afraid if she stared at the grotesquely swelled foot of one, or the carved and wrinkled face of another, that she might feel guilty.

But she was safe in the entrance lobby, guarded by a short stout man in a red jacket and a woman behind glass who sold tickets. Here Olivia felt another stab of uncertainty. She had promised Miranda only to go a little way down La Rambla. Would she be missed at the hostel? Would Miranda worry and call their mom? But the woman behind glass and the man in the red jacket were staring at her, so she handed over five euro and took the plunge.

In the nave, her eyes turned nervously to a floor crossed by fragments of colored light, and she didn't see Mr. Brown ambling toward her until he was already there.

"I didn't know you were coming to the Cathedral today," he said with cheerful surprise. "I thought your sister wanted you to stay near the hostel."

"I got a little lost," she said.

"Well, you're with us now. No harm, no foul."

Olivia smiled tightly, and did not know what to say.

"Do you want to come with us?" Mr. Brown continued, his gray face crinkling around the mouth. "Greg is on the roof, and I was just going to catch up with him."

"There's a roof? I mean, you can go up there? Is that legal?"

"Of course it's legal—it's recommended! And it's completely safe. Come up, or you'll regret it. The view is inspiring. You can see the water."

So Olivia followed Mr. Brown past the choir stalls (whose architectural vintage she couldn't remember) and several gated altars (whose dates she couldn't remember), under the cupola (whose height she couldn't remember), and into an alcove, and then to a small anteroom, and then the elevator, which creaked and took its rusty time, making Olivia anxious.

Olivia's eyes had been dazzled when she entered the Cathedral, and only in the elevator had they eventually become adjusted to the low light. But when the elevator arrived at the top, the door opened on a different side, and stepping into the blinding sunshine, Olivia had no idea where she had turned, what she saw, or who formed the impressions crowding upon her.

Vision returned. In front of her was the castellated top of a tower, a curve of red-shingled roof, and an insubstantial-looking scaffold that screeched and groaned as tourists clattered up and down it.

Her pulse thudded to the tempo of the earlier bells. She looked over her shoulder. Another narrow prominence blocked her view, but between it and the wall, a brilliant red glimpse of Barcelona peeked through.

"Walk up with me. It's perfectly safe," Mr. Brown said.

She took Mr. Brown's hand—the scaffolding was safe but the railing didn't bear his weight comfortably—and they ascended. A catwalk broached the peak of the roof and on the opposite side from the tallest, most jagged spire, a platform allowed visitors to sit and take in the view. Beyond that platform was an inaccessible roof, and then the roofs of other buildings piled up between the mountains, and then, behind a thin haze, the Mediterranean Sea.

"Look, there's Greg," said his father.

And there was Greg, leaning easily on the rail, the breeze blowing his hair back from his eyes, looking farther out than there was anything to see. His ease calmed Olivia. Mr. Brown, now leaning on Olivia's arm, drifted toward him happily.

"Greg, look who I found downstairs. She's all alone today."

Greg smiled briefly and then looked down and strode to the other end of the catwalk.

"He doesn't mean to be rude," Mr. Brown said with a sigh. "He just wants to be alone."

"That's okay, I don't mind," Olivia replied, though she did mind.

"Well, I mind," Mr. Brown said, nudging in on her thoughts. "I worry about him when he does that."

"Oh." Olivia attempted indifference for a moment, but curiosity edged it out, and she finally asked, "Why?"

"Because *he* worries. And people your age shouldn't worry."

"We have things to worry about," Olivia said. "I mean, there's things in the news. Miranda's always telling me to watch the news." She trailed off.

"How old are you?" Mr. Brown turned to her. "Eighteen? Greg's eighteen."

"Yeah."

"And you come from a good house, I bet."

"I guess. What does that mean?"

"You see, that's all relative," he said. "I don't mean to pry. But if I mention one bad thing that's happened to Greg, you'll think of three worse things that have happened to you or someone you know, and none of that's my business either, but you'd tell me."

Olivia thought about it, and answered quietly, "No. I wouldn't do that."

Mr. Brown considered her, and his eyes said plainly that he believed her. But then, abruptly, he said, "Why do young people go to such lengths to make misery a sport?"

"We don't all do that," Olivia said defensively. She felt her palms begin to sweat again. Her breath was short.

"No. But everyone wants to prove they've suffered more. And no one really listens. So Greg stopped talking."

"Greg doesn't talk?"

"Of course Greg talks. Just not about anything important," said Mr. Brown. "None of the things that make him worry and want to be alone."

"Everyone's unhappy sometimes."

"Yes, but not everybody's miserable about it," Mr. Brown said.

There was a building between the cathedral and the sea with a columned belvedere on top, surrounded by potted palms. Another roof showcased an elaborate garden of trailing vines and arbors. Directly below, if Olivia craned over the scaffolding and squinted past the edge of the roof, she could see down into the courtyards surrounding the church. Somewhere down there sat the accordion player.

"Are you happy?" Mr. Brown asked. Olivia snapped her head up sharply.

"What?"

"Are you having a good time?"

"Yeah. I am. But I'm going downstairs now."

"Do you want me to come with you? Or Greg?"

"No, I'll be fine. I'll see you at the hostel." She didn't want to be around Greg when he made it so obvious he didn't want to be around her, and she didn't want to be around his father, who seemed to be searching her soul. It made her uncomfortable.

Olivia hurried down the scaffold as quickly as she felt was safe, and while she waited for the elevator, she stared at the wall as if to examine some minute inscription there, to avoid looking up and seeing Mr. Brown again.

But when she returned to the nave, the pipe organ murmuring without melody reminded her of the accordion music twining atonally with the pealing of the bells. It was like listening to the stones in eerie conversation, and their old tuneless voices reminded her of her journey through the streets. Then the mammoth columns became rippled tree trunks, and she stretched her hand to touch one. She thought about what Mr. Brown had said about worrying, and she wondered what she had been worried about earlier when she first stepped inside. But then she shook off her thoughts about the Browns to focus on grasping this feeling, this now.

Olivia made a lazy circuit and then found the cloister outside, with a dim green garden enclosed in the center. A small fountain with drinking taps filled the cool quadrangle with natural music. Inside the garden fence, geese clattered to each other, and Olivia watched them eat lettuce. Then she purchased three postcards and an informative guide to the cathedral in the gift shop tucked between two chapels, and emerged into the sun once more.

While she had been inside, the day had slipped by, and Olivia realized by the tolling of the bells and the grumbling of her stomach that it must be late in the afternoon. With a resurgence of panic that seemed to have been held in check by the walls of the Cathedral, she remembered her promise to Miranda and wondered what her sister had done all day. She set off in what she hoped was the direction of a larger street that might have a sign pointing her toward La Rambla. The shady afternoon light made the shadows cooler, and warm spots of orange light seemed to float above her reach.

This time, Olivia didn't have to walk far before an unexpected square opened before her from unsuspicious, narrow, gritty streets. This square was cleaner and emptier of adornment than the others she had passed through that day, two ends dominated by blocky buildings with glaring statues guarding their doors. Its starkness arrested her. For a flashing moment, the totally empty square reminded her of the space inside her mind the morning she had laid on her bed, the van waiting outside, everyone sounding so scared.

Olivia couldn't stay. Her stomach whined and fears of upsetting Miranda pierced the memory, which dissipated as quickly as it had arrived. She dragged her feet away, suddenly aware they were swollen and tired. Sure enough, she soon found a sign on the other side of the square which led her back to La Rambla.

As she walked, she wondered what made her so uncomfortable about Mr. Brown's kindness, and why she couldn't stop thinking about their encounter. The more Olivia wanted to stop thinking about it, the harder it became to forget, as she fought her way north through the crowds of blue-shirted Scottish football fans until the buildings grew younger and the signs brighter, and a large raucous noise became louder.

She had found the Plaça Catalunya, the large plaza straddling La Rambla that encircled a fountain in the center of Barcelona, right between the Gothic Quarter and the city's nineteenth-century district. Just a few blocks north on La Rambla was Casa Joven and a bed Olivia's feet screamed for.

Across the street from the Plaça Catalunya, she saw the source of the noise. A mob of Scottish football fans had formed a brick wall, though one that rippled and sang, and somewhere in the center, someone waved a *really* big flag. They'd collected here for no discernible reason, and before the first fan could struggle out, more and more poured in, until the crowd sustained itself, and no one was sure why they were all standing there, except that maybe it would result in victory. Potato chip bags and crushed beer cans paved the sidewalk, and the scent of both hung heavily in the warm air. Once again, Olivia thought momentarily she heard singing in Spanish, or maybe some ancient language, but now she knew it was only drunken Scottish.

The sound and the smells and the way the declining sun now gleamed into the corner of her eye, making her squint, heightened a headache lurking in her brain. She was tired of waiting for the pedestrian signal, but just as she elevated a foot over the curb, a taxi sped around the corner and whipped past her so close she felt its wind. Olivia stepped back as if slapped on the face, waited miserably with everyone else, and then crossed with the pack toward Plaça Catalunya.

Around the central clot of fans, the rest of Plaça Catalunya was crowded as well, a more mobile crowd, and Olivia tried to skirt the worst of it, getting jostled even more violently when she tried to break from the current. Frustratingly, the backs of her shoes were stepped on, twice. When she saw open space toward the fountain in the center of Plaça Catalunya, she elbowed her way toward it.

She was nearly out when a hand on her shoulder stopped her, and she turned around. A grinning, unfamiliar face stared into hers. "Sorry, wrong person," the man said, almost inaudibly, in a thick Scottish accent. Olivia shrugged nervously, and while her head was turned, her bags were ripped out of her hand—her souvenir bags complete with postcards and booklet and the mask she had bought with music on it. She was so squeezed and tumbled by the crowd she couldn't turn back to glimpse who had her things, and when she shouted, no one paid any attention to another noisy carouser in the crowd. Two footballers who saw her grinned, thinking it was some kind of joke.

Holding her purse to her breast (and feeling, with relief, her wallet still secure in the hidden zippered pocket inside, and her book), Olivia tried to elbow her way out of the crowd, tripping and stomping on her own share of innocent bystanders, finding that no matter where she spun, she seemed to be pointing directly toward the center of the fray. She saw an empty space ahead, like the eye of a storm, and made an open break for it.

Just as suddenly, she stopped. The clearing was formed by a circle of people standing on the pavement around a man with a bloody grin, a crimson pool around his head. Several people on their knees pushed him back down every time he tried to get up, laughing, though Olivia had no idea what was so funny. A crew of medics cracked through the storm of people with a stretcher to whisk away the drunk.

For a moment, the circle of people opened and the man on the ground looked directly at Olivia. His front tooth was missing.

Mesmerized and disgusted, she felt the same claustrophobic dread creep over her she thought she'd banished that day in August she'd finally clawed her way out of the chasm of her mind. She felt the paralysis creeping up her legs.

But then a voice by her side broke through and, like a summer mist, dispelled the anxiety.

"He'll be okay. The guy's really sorry for hitting him. I heard him," said Greg Brown. "Come on, we can get out this way."

She felt his hand around her shoulder. From the spot where he touched her spread a warmth that thawed her immobility, and when they were far enough away that the circle closed again and the bloody man was out of sight, it spread to a weak, relieved smile. She saw that he too was relieved.

"How did you get here?" she asked.

"Same way as you. Unless you swam or flew."

Olivia smiled, and from the tautness of her face, she realized that a few tears had rolled down her cheek a few moments earlier. Sometimes she felt like a sink on the verge of overflowing. She tried to pretend to yawn so she could cover her face and wipe the tears away, but it turned into a real yawn. Greg laughed a little.

"Wanna go back?" he asked her.

"No, actually," Olivia said, surprising herself. "Not anymore. Miranda's going to give me an earful, so I might as well put it off as long as I can."

"Let's get a snack, then."

"Where's your dad?"

"He went back ahead of me," said Greg. "I wanted to stay out."

"The day is almost over."

"Only the afternoon."

"I like the sun here," said Olivia.

"Sit down and I'll get us some coffee."

Olivia sat on the edge of the fountain. An old woman and an adolescent walked by. After a few minutes, Greg came back with coffee and pretzels from a touristy stall in the corner of the square. He gave one of each to Olivia, his hand touching hers casually.

"Spanish pretzels?" she asked.

"I guess."

"Whatever."

In the late afternoon light, Greg Brown looked happy, and that looked good on him. Olivia looked away quickly.

They ate quietly. Olivia looked at her hands, the food, the inside of the coffee cup, the ground under her feet. When she was done, she looked at the crumpled napkin in her hand, and then she looked up. She wanted to ask him what was wrong.

"Someone took my stuff," she said with a sigh.

"What?"

"I was in the crowd and someone grabbed my bags right out of my hands," Olivia said.

"What did you have?"

"Some stuff I bought. Some postcards. And a mask."

"A mask? Why'd you buy a mask?"

"It was pretty."

"Oh," said Greg. "That's too bad."

"I really liked the mask," Olivia said.

"Well, it's gone now," he said, standing. "So just let it go." He stood awkwardly for a few beats. "Anyway, I found you," he said finally. He offered her his hand. She stood without grabbing it.

The singing in the square had continued all that time, but it didn't grate on Olivia anymore. Instead, she let it wash over her, like the afternoon light, as the crowd moved and blurred. She and Greg walked slowly, but she felt as if she was walking in place, and the scene was slowly revolving toward her. Their rhythm was gentle and gradual, and Olivia noticed, looking down, that her feet had fallen into step with Greg's, unless his had adjusted to hers first.

They stopped at a crossing and waited for the light.

Olivia stared at the building opposite, geometric and mesmerizing, until she became self-aware again. Something warm pricked on her neck. She looked up at Greg. Greg was looking at her.

The light changed, but Olivia couldn't move. She didn't want to move. Greg met her gaze steadily, with warmth, like the warmth she felt on her neck—not unpleasant, but new. She wanted to ask him why he had been there. She wanted to ask him why he had smiled and walked toward her, when earlier he had seen her and strode away.

The green man disappeared from the pedestrian light, Greg snatched her hand, and they ran clean across just as the next wave of cars began to move.

4

THEYS OF WE

It was Miranda who had been more thoroughly lost that day. She had had no bells to guide her.

That morning, she and Lenny had dashed into the Plaça del Rei just in time to attach themselves to the rear end of the Gothic Quarter walking tour—at least they thought it was the Gothic Quarter walking tour, until twenty minutes and many winding alleys later, the group descended into a sandwich bar, and they realized it was just a large family party with a vociferous and well-researched matriarch. Lenny laughed.

"That was fucking brilliant!" she screamed to Miranda. "I can't believe we just did that!"

"Now I have to go back and check everything in my guidebook," Miranda said. "What if what she said wasn't right? Let's just go back and catch the next real tour."

"Don't worry, I know everything," Lenny said. "We'll just wander around here, where the Jensons dropped us—hey, Paolo!"

Lenny promptly left Miranda to join a man leaning against a wall down the way. Miranda kept her distance at first, but eventually she strode briskly to join Lenny when it became obvious her companion had no idea she was fuming.

She might as well have waited. Lenny and Paolo were talking in Catalan, a regional language slightly different from Spanish, and despite a quick nod to acknowledge Miranda's arrival, Lenny didn't switch to English or make any attempt to involve Miranda in the conversation. Even Paolo seemed slightly uncomfortable, darting quick curious looks at Lenny's unintroduced friend.

Lenny spoke with the speed of fluency, but with an unapologetically bold Anglicized accent. Paolo's answers were, to Miranda's ears, brief and gruff. His eyes sparkled a little, slyly, as if with amusement, but he made no move to invite the ladies somewhere more comfortable than the slightly garbage-smelling alley.

After about ten minutes, the conversation ended, Lenny slapping Paolo on the rear in a gesture that made both Miranda and Paolo visibly uncomfortable. The women walked away, Lenny taking the lead; behind them, a shuffle and a snap signaled Paolo lighting a cigarette.

"That was my buddy Paolo," said Lenny. "He owns a bar just around the corner. Met him on my last visit here. Pure Barcelona, all the way back to medieval fishermen. But I'm glad I know where we are now, 'cause now I know where we have to go to get lost."

"You're kidding, right?" Miranda said, and when Lenny didn't reply, she optimistically believed she *was* kidding, until, sixteen blocks later, they were well and undeniably lost.

"I love this city," Lenny said as they strode along. Lenny was a strong walker and Miranda had to jog to keep up. "It's so real. The locals here are so laid-back. Not as tight-assed as the French, way sexier than the English, bathe more than the Italians. If I could bring myself to settle in any one place, it would be Barcelona. Or Tibet."

Miranda believed that any place not filled with tourists must be even more dangerous than the places filled with tourists. Miranda did not like danger. The belt-bag and sweater-tied crowds thinned, and at length they found themselves in a grim alley of boarded-up shops, two bars, and a dumpster. Instead of being surrounded by blushing stone, it was gritty brick and concrete. Miranda protested that they were now in the part of the city where Spanish people actually lived.

"Great. Check it out—this is where they go to work, go to school, buy their groceries. I love finding the real city. And I bet there isn't another American for blocks. I hate traveling Americans. They're so fucking loud all the time." Lenny turned to Miranda and noticed a hurt look on her face. "I know. It gets to you, too. But you're better than that—you're from Virginia. You understand history."

"Maybe we should look for a Metro station," Miranda said.

"No, I wanna make a few friends. Look at that sandwich bar there. Cute. They have a neon sign."

"I don't speak Spanish," Miranda said. "Well, I mean, I did, a little, once, but I let it go."

"Well, I'm going if you're not."

Miranda was not, though Lenny didn't wait long to find out. Instead, Miranda at last whipped out her map without shame, found the closest main street, and then the nearest Metro station. Six stops later, she emerged from the Plaça Catalunya Metro.

Outside, in the plaza, a seething crowd was growing, and Miranda walked briskly past it and up the street, slipped into the hostel, and felt, for the first time that day, that her money or virtue wasn't about to be snatched by the dirty, desperate men who inhabit every darkened doorframe in every large city outside Virginia.

She was slightly relieved to find that her sister wasn't waiting, or watching. She would have to make sure Olivia never went out with Lenny alone.

Retiring to their private room for the first time, Miranda was taken aback to find, pinned to the wall, a thin sheet of notebook paper. On it was written only a question mark. *It had to have been left by that mopey-looking son of Mr. Brown, Greg. Who else had been in the room and could have left it?* Miranda couldn't imagine Hugo doing something so strange it would frighten customers, and for the same reason she didn't suspect the blond girl.

It had to be Greg. He probably thought he was some kind of tortured soul. He probably had a tattoo, or some weird piercing she couldn't see.

Miranda was overtaken by her protective instinct once again. A month ago, Olivia had found an old toy buried in the backyard and wouldn't talk to anyone for a week. What if Greg had left more question marks hidden in their room? What if Olivia discovered one, and found it so strange and unexpected that it set her off again?

Irritated, Miranda rushed toward the paper and tore it down, crumpled it, and let it drop from her hands to the floor. How much weirder could Greg Brown get—or his dad, for that matter? She couldn't believe she was staying in *their* old room.

Miranda left the room, telling herself she simply wanted to browse the pamphlets and bulletin board in the common area. After glancing over the material there, she settled on a couch to look at her own guidebook. As she leafed through it, a short, bright-looking man clambered in the door with a cheerful nod to Hugo. He looked like he could be in his late twenties, and was dressed with a warm practicality and unobtrusive hints of fashion. Miranda approved. What she noticed particularly was his scarf—plaid, knotted around his neck—even though he didn't wear a jacket.

He spotted her, leaned forward, squinted, and came toward her.

"Are you Olivia's sister?" he said. "Your faces have the same shape."

"Yes. I'm Miranda."

"Marc. I met Olivia this morning. She's very sweet." He sat down beside her and slipped out of his bag's strap.

"Oh," said Miranda. She was taken aback slightly. "She's the sweetest girl in the world."

"You sound like her mom."

"There's an age difference."

"Oh, well," Marc said. "So you're from Virginia, I hear."

"That's true."

"I come from Lima." He ended with a tight smile.

Miranda nodded and tried to figure out what could give this person such an air of being interesting before he managed to say anything interesting about himself.

"So. What do you do there?" she asked.

"I'm preparing to take religious orders," he said.

"Oh," she squeaked, drawing it out longer than she'd intended. That *was* interesting. Priests interested her, especially young ones—she couldn't figure out why. It was something old-fashioned, or comforting, non-threatening. But conversationally, she remained at a loss.

"Do you know the Browns?" she asked.

"The Browns? Everyone wants to know about the Browns today. Your sister already asked."

Miranda was not happy about that. Why would Olivia be interested in the Browns? She didn't want Olivia to be interested in anyone who forced them to change rooms in the morning or left creepy question marks all over like a weird emo calling card.

"What do you know about them?" she asked.

"They're from the South," Marc said. "They don't waste time when they think they're doing good. The father is nice enough, but the son seems a little broody."

"Broody? That's putting it lightly. I found a question mark on my wall. I think Greg put it there."

Marc only grinned.

"Oh, that's the kind of thing teenagers do," he said. "You were one, too. I bet you had something you wrote or wore or did to show the world how mad you were at it, right?"

After that, Miranda didn't know what to do with her animosity. She stewed for a moment, then broke in with more questions.

"But what do they do?" Miranda said. "Why are they here?"

"Sightseeing, I assume. I think the father is some kind of preacher— not my church. Perhaps one of those large ones you see on American television. Evangelical or something. But he's very well-meaning. The son seems like a follower. When I squint, I can see him leading a flock in about ten years." Marc chuckled dryly. "They're typical Appalachian. Very handy. They fixed the tap in the back bathroom the first night they arrived. Hugo offered them a discount and the father waved it off."

"I'm surprised Hugo did that much. He's out for all he can get," Miranda grumbled, half to herself. Marc seemed amused.

"They're really very nice people," he said. "Painfully nice, you know? I think everyone's a little too afraid. If they stand too close to them, eventually they'll be thrown into a river and baptized."

Miranda smiled and rolled her eyes with him. Marc was the kind of priest she liked best—cosmopolitan, not pushy, not too religious all the time. She couldn't imagine a TV preacher being this urbane.

"I left your little sister behind this morning when she very much wanted to go out," said Marc, standing. "Can I make it up by taking the elder sister to some tapas?" With obvious affectation, he straightened his shoulders.

Miranda was delighted. If Olivia came back while they were gone, she would probably just read her book until Miranda returned.

They settled on a tapas café down the block, and after Miranda's cautions against sidewalk purse-snatchers and the late-autumn surge of insects (which she had read about, and was sure would make itself felt anytime now), they sat inside.

"Now, you must tell me what brings you to this part of the world," Marc said with a grin as he shook out his napkin.

"Well, I'd heard it was a beautiful place, and I've already done Madrid," said Miranda. "And, well, you understand why people come to Spain."

Marc nodded. "But why not in the spring?" he asked. "I would have come in the spring if I'd had the time. I came once when I was a little boy, and it was magical."

Miranda explained her mother's views on Thanksgiving—something about cultural oppression and nationalistic holidays—and the need to get Olivia out of the house. Something in her wanted to add how the whole house had seemed to remind Olivia of her childhood so strongly she hadn't been able to let go of it—how she'd seemed obsessed with the ghost of the child she used to be. "I didn't know how to appreciate it when I was little," Olivia had told her with a weak smile, holding up whatever young adult novel she'd been rereading when Miranda stopped by the house for the weekend. Miranda always had the sense that Olivia hadn't just been talking about the book.

But Miranda said nothing.

"And what do you do?" Marc asked.

"I do accounting at Friendly Neighbor Insurance. Their corporate headquarters." Miranda paused. "My sister's taking a year off before starting at Cornell. A lot of people do it, especially in Europe, I think." Miranda thought again about what their mother had said when she'd mentioned her plan to go to Barcelona: that it would "culturally enhance Olivia's interface with her surroundings." Miranda had just hoped it would inspire, well, *any* interaction between Olivia and the world. She'd felt she was losing her sister somewhere inside her sister.

"You have a very prestigious family."

"So you'd think. But some of our neighbors don't like that Olivia is going north. I guess it can't be helped—a lot of smart kids don't get into Cornell, you know."

"I see."

"Personally, I think it'd be good for the Somersets to leave the South," said Miranda. "I've always thought so. Maybe up there, Olivia can really learn about important things. Like politics."

"Does she follow the issues much?"

"No, not at all. It's embarrassing sometimes."

"Well, she'll grow into it," said Marc.

"She's old enough. She just needs to learn how to care about these things," said Miranda. "At least our mom is progressive, even if she's a little . . . eccentric. Better her kind of crazy than Stepford Wives, I guess. She married into the South, but she kept her name and supported herself." She didn't mention their father had split when Olivia was too young to remember him, or that he was now dead. The only thing he had left them was his name.

Marc made a politely interested noise.

"Well, she was a pioneer for her time," Miranda said.

Their drinks arrived, followed by a plate of roasted peppers.

"That's one thing I can't stand about these tapas places—the food just trickles in," Miranda said. "Can't they fill an order all at once? It was the same when I went to Madrid two years ago."

Marc's best response was a sigh and a shake of the head, and then they toasted to Barcelona.

At the end of the meal, Marc reached for the bill and Miranda loudly protested, insisting they split it. After a few awkward moments spent calculating tip and exchanging big bills for littler ones, they rose and walked back to the hostel.

When they returned, Miranda noted with somewhat more alarm

than before that Olivia was not waiting for her. In fact, it was long past Olivia and Miranda's usual lunchtime—she and Marc had eaten late and leisurely. When Olivia finally entered, followed by none other than Greg Brown, Miranda was bristling. It was late afternoon.

"Where the hell have you been? I was this close to calling the police!" Miranda began in a low but forceful tone, right there in the common room. Olivia slipped out of her shoes by the door. Her ears turned red while her sister continued. "How was I supposed to know you weren't murdered on the street? You could have become one of those people you read about back home! I can't believe this from you, Olivia!"

"I got lost," Olivia said, wavering between statement and question.

"How can you get lost on one street that goes straight?" Miranda said.

"I saw something I liked," Olivia said, sitting on one of the couches and looking at her empty hands.

"Well, from this moment on, you are going absolutely nowhere alone," said Miranda. "If I see so much as the tip of your nose outside this hostel's door alone, I'm calling Mom."

Olivia looked up sharply.

"Are you going to tell her about today?" she asked.

Miranda turned away from her.

"No," she answered at length. "Because I thought you'd be responsible enough to handle yourself. But that was my mistake, and now you have fair warning."

Greg, who until now had lingered awkwardly and apologetically near the door, slid away to his dorm room without a word.

Olivia looked for something to warm the chill that had fallen over the room.

"Look," she said. "There are flowers here. There weren't flowers here this morning."

There hadn't been. But now, a tall vase with four graceful, succulent lilies sat upon one of the two dining tables.

Hugo was washing dishes in the kitchen (though no matter how many lazy swipes he made with the cloth, no dishes seemed to leave the sink, and none appeared on the drying rack). Apparently, he understood English better when it was spoken by Olivia, because he pointed to the flowers and said, "Emery." At their blank looks, he added, "Mr. Brown."

He shook one dish and seemed to consider putting it on the drying rack, but then set it down on the bottom of the sink again, dried his hands, and dove into a box of crackers. "He gave them to Sophie," Hugo continued when he saw Olivia still paying attention. "She said yesterday she wanted more flowers, and he asked which she liked."

"He's speaking English," Miranda spat under her breath as Hugo wandered away. "Unbelievable. Is this just a game he plays with people he doesn't like?"

Olivia didn't reflect on Hugo's spotty record of understanding or ignoring English speakers. Instead, she imagined Mr. Brown looking for lilies in the stalls on the street. She could even see him apologizing that they were only greenhouse flowers, as if, had he the power, he would cause it to be spring so she could have flowers grown in the full freedom of the sun. No, better yet, she imagined him placing flowers quietly on the table in the deserted room and wandering away, leaving them to be discovered.

Sophie, the blond girl who helped Hugo, was at her usual seat at the back computer. As Olivia looked at her profile this afternoon, she thought she saw something softer around her eyes, or the region of her nose. Her mouth remained compressed in a strict line, but she did flick her eyes once toward Olivia, and nodded to her almost imperceptibly.

Could the flowers have done this to her? Or was it Mr. Brown who wove these changes with gentle hands?

Olivia retrieved her book from her bag and planted herself on the common room couch. Miranda paced in front of her, but she seemed to have lost the thread of her rant.

"Olivia!" Miranda snapped. "Don't think this conversation is over." Olivia looked up, sincerely contrite, but then her eyes returned to her book. "Go pick up your stuff," Miranda said. She leaned forward and spoke a little lower. "That door is always open," she said, tossing a glance over her shoulder at the front door, ajar and guarded by the empty reception desk.

Olivia sighed and set down her book. When she rose, Miranda took her place on the couch with a huff. Olivia gathered her purse, jacket, and shoes, and carried them obediently out of the common space, watched gravely by Sophie from her computer hideout in the back of the room.

Sophie pattered over to her lilies and straightened them in their vase. Then she drifted into the kitchen, where Hugo said something loud and friendly. She replied in dry, indifferent words, which Miranda recognized but could not understand.

In the cool eddy of her private room, apart from the noisy stream of the rest of the hostel, Olivia put away her things and breathed deeply, trying to recall the solemn peacefulness she found in *A Wrinkle in Time*. But it was impossible to think of flying horses and time monsters when reality lay so closely by. There were gargoyles in this city, and phantasms of musicians, and masqued balls, and great sleeping dragons. Free from Miranda, but still watched by Miranda's looming suitcase, Olivia sat on her bed and removed the detritus from her bag. A ticket. A receipt. A few coins that looked the same.

On the floor, a bit of trash caught her eye, and she picked it up and uncrinkled it. A question mark stared back at her. She traced it with her finger—it was Greg's. She knew just by touching it. She turned the sheet to see if there was anything on the back.

my father moved through dooms of love, it said. Olivia rolled the phrase around in her mouth silently. It whispered dryly in and out of her lips.

my father moved through dooms of love

Following the sort of impulse she never shared with her sister, her mother, or any of her few friends (gone now to far-flung universities, like a peaceful population scattered by the appearance of an ogre), she folded the battered sheet carefully and tucked it into the bottom of her backpack. Searching the pockets of the jeans she'd worn yesterday, she found the handkerchief she had never returned and placed it there as well. She knew Mr. Brown would never ask for its return.

Olivia eased back onto her bed, and as the pressure lifted from the bottoms of her feet, she felt momentarily weightless, which triggered an instant and fleeting smile. She swung her legs up lazily, crossed them on the bed, and folded her arms under her head.

Across the hall, past a haphazardly open door at the end of the long rows of beds and beyond their hanging towels, Greg Brown reclined in the same position in the bunk by the window. He dreamed that the scent of lilies filled the air.

Miranda had told Olivia that one hour of jetlag is recovered each day of a person's stay in a new time zone. Olivia calculated that she would feel perfectly rested by the day they planned to leave. Greg didn't calculate, but simply dropped into a deep sleep.

When Hugo came by, whistling, his hands in his pockets, he softly closed each of their doors, knowing what commotion would begin as his guests returned and began making dinner and dinner plans. The silence germinated Olivia's dreams and Greg's, until they grew green tendrils which slipped under their doors and sinuously twined in the glow of the hanging lamp in the common room. His dreams and her dreams tangled in a jungle of fresh sensation, and from them grew lilies—lilies under the feet of Miranda as she sat on the couch with her guidebook, making small marks on places of interest; the feet of Marc, while he read from his small notebook and ate a fresh pastry at one of the tables; the feet of Sophie, making coffee, pulsating lyrics in her head.

The only person who noticed the vegetation was Mr. Brown, and then only barely, determining that it was the lilies on the table releasing a lovely scent.

Behind Olivia's eyes, the world was green. She tossed with the motion of her thoughts until the creaking of the springs below her woke her, horrified at what her mind had created. Struggling to shake free, she rose, headachy and discontented.

That evening, dinner took place in the common room, and both Somersets attended. However, Miranda insisted they cook their own food, and so Olivia waited at a table with Lenny and Marc, and while they ate, Miranda boiled a small portion of pasta for herself and Olivia. Marc was flicking through a magazine while Lenny half-heartedly scribbled on a small notebook during pauses in the conversation, or when others were too busy preparing food to talk. The Browns had gone out to eat with a Polish couple who had just arrived. Language was apparently no barrier given a shared love of gardening.

"They just invited themselves along," Lenny opined. "It's like they can't leave people alone. Maybe they think they'll convert them. They say grace, you know, before dinner." Lenny paused before continuing. "At least, the dad does. I have no idea what goes on in that kid's head."

"Ana and Chas didn't seem to mind," Marc said with a smile. "It's very brave for people to attempt communication with so few common words between them. Not many people are even brave enough to try to learn a second language." Almost as an afterthought, he added, "And they say grace silently."

"I used to speak a little Spanish, but I let most of it go. And Olivia and

I both took French for two years in middle school," Miranda said, setting down two plates of tortellini and sitting beside her sister.

"You've been to France?" Marc asked.

"No."

"Well, I don't think the Browns are the bilingual type," Lenny said with a sneer. "They think they're quite the little heroes for stunts like the flower thing. It's like, you know, they're trying to prove they're holier than thou."

Olivia didn't see how it was like that at all, but her throat tightened up when she thought about speaking up.

"It's like the room thing!" Miranda said, jumping in. "Thinking they're doing us this big favor, but really just being awkward and strange."

Lenny snickered. Olivia went white. Her heart hammered harder, and she thought of the piece of paper she had found on the floor. She wondered if Miranda had seen it, and if Miranda had been the one to crumple and discard it.

"I saw Mr. Brown at the Cathedral of Barcelona today," Olivia said quietly.

"You went all the way to the Cathedral? I thought we were going to go together, Olivia!"

"Only for a little. I—I didn't see much."

"Yeah, I bet Greg was trying to carve lyrics into one of the columns or some shit like that," Lenny said. "I hate emo kids. Angst à la redneck. I bet he wore eyeliner in high school and can't figure out how to tell his dad he's coming out of the closet." She stopped for a second to snicker. "I'd love to see that."

"I saw him in a really flattering shade of green today," Marc said. "It was the same color as leaves in the springtime."

Olivia could only think of Greg on the roof, awash in sunlight.

"Do you know the line 'my father moved through dooms of love'?"

Olivia asked suddenly.

"It's an E. E. Cummings poem," said Marc.

"Oh yeah, it just sounds like him, doesn't it?" Lenny said. "E. E.'s the man. I really love him, especially that one in the Woody Allen movie—the one that makes the girl cry—"

"'somewhere i have never travelled, gladly beyond,'" Marc said. "*Hannah and Her Sisters*."

Lenny nodded and smiled tightly. It struck Olivia that Lenny wasn't actually too happy that someone else enjoyed the same movies as her. It was as if she wanted to be the only one who liked that stuff.

"Okay. Thanks," Olivia whispered in the silence.

"I think Mr. Brown was reading some Cummings here earlier," Marc said. "I'm sure he'd lend it to you."

"Seriously?" Lenny cried. "Really? I didn't think they were into . . . reading. You know, the first night I was here, he told the whole room he never went to college. I figured, okay, whatever, he's just a product of his time and place. But with the internet and new schools and stuff, there's absolutely no excuse for him not to give Greg a shot at education, you know? I mean, who in this day and age doesn't go to college? You'd think he'd just want to get out of wherever they live, right? But I asked him where he was going to college and he said he hadn't applied anywhere, and he was just thinking of taking classes at the community college until he 'figures it out.' Like staying in whatever backwater they're from is going to offer him any great insights. I bet his dad helps censor the local library," she said. "Anyway, that was the first night, and after he told me that, he just wandered off like an idiot and didn't say anything to me again."

"Where's his mom?" Olivia asked softly.

"I think she's dead," Marc said.

Olivia's breath caught. Why did she suddenly feel guilty?

Everyone else at the table indulged the simultaneous urge to stuff their faces. But before Lenny could interpret this as encouragement to continue, Marc swallowed hard and leaned toward Miranda.

"So, what are your plans for tomorrow?" he asked a little too brightly.

"We could do Gaudí tomorrow," Miranda said.

"Okay," said Olivia, ready to agree with anything that would set her feet moving, as if that could stop her mind from spinning.

"A full day would give you more time to stay and look at the things you like," Marc said.

"I guess you could always add a few more sights to fill it out, unless you really want to use up a whole day on it," Lenny said with a sigh.

Olivia suddenly looked up to Marc and said, "Come with us."

"Well, I was only going to wander tomorrow anyway, so I guess I can wander with you, if you'll take me," he said, with some hesitation.

"I guess I can come along too," Lenny said without invitation.

Before Lenny could propose leading the group, Miranda spoke of the works she wanted to see—the Casa Milá, the Sagrada Familia, and the Casa Batlló. "That should be enough for a whole day," she said.

"Or more," Marc said. He beamed charmingly at Miranda. "You'd better gather your strength."

That evening, Olivia raided the stock of guidebooks she shared with Miranda to read up on Antoni Gaudí. She wanted to be an expert by tomorrow. She wanted to do tomorrow so much better than she had done today.

Lenny sought the companionship of a few Scottish football fans—two or three, if she was lucky—who were probably the coolest tourists around, way more laid-back than the English, and definitely with sexier accents.

Marc took a stroll down La Rambla for some fresh(er) air and returned to write in his journal.

Miranda, with her usual efficiency, managed to wear herself out between washing up and corresponding with friends at home, but waited to go to bed until ten o'clock. Following her own jet-lag rule, she sat stubbornly upright in a computer chair in front of her e-mail, nodding off every five minutes.

Olivia read, lying on her bed, until Miranda came in to sleep and turned out the light. Olivia lay awake until all was silent. Worn out on Gaudí before she had even seen his buildings in real life, she slipped into the common room to lose herself in *A Wrinkle in Time*.

But the room wasn't deserted yet. When she rounded the corner, she saw Hugo and Sophie close together on one of the couches. Hugo slouched back, and Sophie leaned into him, one hand lazily weaving through his hair, the other settled in the crook of his elbow, her thumb stroking his arm. Hugo held her loosely around her waist, with a lazy grin subtly different from the one he showed all the guests.

Sophie saw her staring and Olivia's heart caught in her throat, but before she could retreat, Sophie rose stiffly, and Hugo alone remained slouched on the couch, relaxed and unembarrassed. When Sophie moved for the door, Hugo stirred fluidly from the couch and followed her. While they said goodbye in the dim foyer, Olivia climbed into the deep chair in the back corner to pretend as visibly as possible that she was invisible.

After Sophie left (a few words, a brief silence, the click of the latch), Hugo returned to Olivia, his old smirk still hanging off the corners of his lips.

"Need anything?" he asked good-naturedly.

"No, I'm fine, thanks, I just came to read my book." Olivia's explanation tumbled over itself. When Hugo remained in place, she added, "I'm sorry I interrupted you."

"It's okay. She's not upset. Just shy." He smiled. For the first time, Olivia saw Sophie as Mr. Brown must have seen her right away—as Hugo knew her to be all along. And now the flowers made perfect sense.

"I hope you have a nice night," Olivia said.

Hugo nodded, then disappeared into the other end of the entrance hall, where Olivia could only assume he lived, though it would be just as natural to assume the kitchen was his home, and the corner of the couch he had just occupied his bed—or that he never slept at all, but continually haunted the places where someone needed a friend. Except Olivia knew that wasn't true. There was more to his existence than hostel guests. Olivia winced, inside and out—not at accidentally walking in on Hugo's date, but at her own surprise that he would have one.

Olivia slid her book between her hands. She liked the feel of its matte cover, ridged where the writing was. Flipping the book's pages, she inhaled the old smell of dusty paper and dusty bookshelves. Sometimes, at home, she would sit for hours without reading at all, just touching her book and dreaming about what was inside it.

Her eyes wandered the room and alighted on the window. Its view was identical to the view from the dorm room on their first night in Barcelona, only twenty-four hours ago, and Olivia observed that, in the moonlight, the garden seemed deeper, while the laundry hanging from rails had disappeared and lights behind curtains shivered and blinked.

On the windowsill, Mr. Brown's book of selected Cummings poems was perched under his folded glasses. With the same thrill she felt opening drawers in her grandparents' house, Olivia picked the book up.

It was an old hardback in faded cloth. It smelled like a library and the typeset was wide and round. Olivia felt the roughness of the pages' edges—cut but not trimmed and smoothed to a uniform width. Cradling it between the moonlight and the red glow of a reading lamp, she looked for and read "my father moved through dooms of love."

The lines were short, but she struggled, picking at each word to find its meaning. Together, they must have been used as a code for other words that formed a logical and complete thought. It was senseless, though. The meaning was coded more thoroughly than she could decipher.

Halfway through, her concentration was interrupted by the appearance of Marc in plaid pajamas.

"Hoo! Hoo!" he hooted, like an owl, pouring himself a glass of water from a bottle in the fridge. He shuffled over to Olivia and peered down at her.

"Feeling all right?" he asked.

"Yeah, just couldn't sleep," she said, tilting her head up.

"Exciting day tomorrow," he said. "Don't wear yourself out now."

"I'll go to bed soon," she said.

Marc tipped the book in her hands up slightly.

"Cummings? Mr. Brown's?" he asked. Olivia nodded. "I heard him and Greg come in with Ana and Chas tonight," Marc said.

"Oh?" said Olivia, suppressing a yawn, though her heart beat faster.

"They were talking about going to Girona tomorrow. They're leaving very early in the morning, or at least Mr. Brown and Ana and Chas are. I was afraid I'd wake them getting up like this, but it's like a greenhouse in there—the room is nearly full, you know."

"Greg's not going?" The words tumbled out of Olivia before she could stop them.

"I'm not sure. He made noises about lingering behind. Knowing him, he'll just slouch off somewhere on his own." Marc lifted an eyebrow but didn't press Olivia on her question. She had the sense she was being cheerfully tolerated, like a little kid who doesn't make much sense but still sounds cute.

Olivia, biting her lip, searched for something else to say.

"It's cool out here," she said.

"Yes, but not really as nice as being in bed," Marc said, laughing. "Goodnight, and I hope you sleep well."

Olivia wished him the same. By now it was clear that Miranda couldn't stand Greg and his father, and that she and Olivia had formed their own little clique with Lenny and Marc. Olivia was used to following her sister, but often suspected that every group but hers was more playful, relaxed, and free.

Though she had never met them, Olivia assumed Ana and Chas from Poland were the paradigm of pleasantness and adventurousness and joyfulness, because Mr. Brown had chosen to go with them to Girona for the day instead of waiting to hear of Olivia's plans. She was surprised by the tiny flicker of jealousy she felt.

The feeling quieted when she looked down and found Cummings open on her lap. She began to read, this time less meticulously, just for the sake of moving her eyes over a text, like stroking the soft blanket she'd had as a child. She let the words flow, and while they now made as little sense to her as before, somehow she felt them more as they dropped into her mind like pellets of rain. Since the afternoon, Sophie's lilies had been moved to the back of the room near the window, away from the places where the guests bustled most. They smelled like green and white.

Olivia rode the word current like the bus through the mountains, strange and new and sleep-drugged. Without quite understanding what the poet had said, she found herself suspended in the resonance of sad remembrance. She felt neither hopeless nor unhappy. The poem's last line struck like a bell, and it rang in varying tones.

love is the whole and more than all
It was written again in a strong hand at the bottom of the page.
love is the whole and more than all

She closed her eyes and she read it again, written on the inside of herself.

love is the whole and more than all

In her dreams, it was followed by Sophie's hand in Hugo's hair; by Marc in plaid pajamas, writing in a small black book; by Miranda the rainy day she left for college; by their mother, entering the library, glancing back, leather bag on her shoulder, her graying flyaway hair a penumbra around the crescent of her cheek.

Or Sophie's hand in Marc's hair, mountains, beggars; Miranda very close to Lenny, shafts of moonlight; Mr. Brown in the Plaça Catalunya, with Ana and Chas, on the other side of a pane of glass, and farther and farther away from them she is borne on a wave of anxious discontent, and she swims against it, and she breaks through—

Greg on the roof of the Cathedral. Greg in the sun and the wind's hand in his hair. Greg's hand around her hand. Lilies.

love is the whole and more than all

5

HE BECKONS

The next morning, Miranda found Olivia in the chair in the corner, a blanket spread across her shoulders. Only a few other guests had crept out very, very quietly, very much earlier that morning, and they had made every attempt to let the girl sleep. The book had been pulled from under her resting palms, closed neatly, and set on the windowsill, without waking her.

From the time when Olivia could still fit neatly in a ball between the armrests, Miranda had seen her little baby sister curled in chairs with forgotten books.

She took Olivia's hand and gently squeezed it, until Olivia's eyes drifted open like globes of a rising sun.

"Why'd you sleep out here?" Miranda asked.

"I guess I just drifted off," Olivia said.

"Did you sleep well?"

"I don't remember waking up at all," Olivia said, groaning softly as she leaned forward. She stretched her arms above her head and felt a satisfying pop.

Olivia couldn't remember her dreams, except in smudges of confusion, and by the time her pupils adjusted to the light, her mind was clear, like waves of morning air. Across her shoulders was a blanket, warm and soft and smelling like old wool and dryer sheets, but she didn't wonder who had draped it there. She only enjoyed the feeling of being taken care of. The dreams, she knew, had come from a line in a poem, and the book caught her eye. In the pragmatic light of morning, she reached for the book and stroked its cover, unafraid.

"Watch it, Olivia's gotten into the E. E. C.," Lenny grumbled as she entered the room. Olivia rose. "She'll be fragmentary all day."

"Olivia!" Miranda exclaimed. "Is that Mr. Brown's book? Were you reading it last night? What if he wanted it? What if he was looking for it?"

"I didn't think he'd mind," Olivia said, noting that while the book had returned to the windowsill, the pastor's glasses had vanished. Olivia creaked toward the hall and bathroom, finding feeling in her knees and ankles again and wishing she hadn't.

"Aren't you going to have some breakfast?" Miranda said.

"I'm taking a shower."

"Don't forget breakfast!"

Breakfast slid from Olivia's mind as she slid out of her clothes and into the water. There were two stalls in the shared ladies' room, and one was occupied, so Olivia took the other one, with a broken shower fixture that wouldn't stay clipped to the wall. She turned it on and held the showerhead by its handle over herself. The water was shockingly cold at first, and she flinched away, a stab of irritation waking her. Then the warm water came, and she sprayed it over herself until her face molded upward into a close-lipped smile.

Olivia knew she should be polite and conserve the water, but other impulses ruled. She recalled afternoons as a child when she'd move and look at each finger and toe individually, totaling twenty distinct, minute actions and inspections—and the evenings when, refusing to turn on the lamp until the last shred of daylight had faded, she would sit immersed in the shifting tide of twilight's blue and gray. With one hand on the showerhead, she used the other to examine every part of her that she could see or reach, even the parts she tried not to think about. She was short, not thin but healthily soft, and, since the age of thirteen, accustomed to ignoring everything below her chin with steady resignation.

In the shower in Barcelona, she extended one arm, and then the other, and flexed her fingers, and peered up along the length of each limb until it looked like a long, fleshy willow branch. She cleaned herself until all the dull parts glowed and the light seemed to come from inside, and she no longer felt her face to be separate from her naked body.

And then she turned the water on her hair, which was long and knotty and wild. It took a few seconds for the steady stream to soak through, and when it did, she leaned her head back and felt her hair's weight pulling her chin up.

Water ran into her ears—she shivered. It streamed in round, galloping rivers down her back, and she curled her toes. The warmth spread across the nape of her neck. When her arms became tired from holding the shower over herself, she turned it off and, hearing silence in the bathroom outside, wrapped her towel on her head and stepped boldly out.

That was a miscalculation. Sophie was there, in front of the mirror, braiding her stick-straight blond hair. Olivia ran back into the shower before she could even blush. Hearing the door open and close, she breathed deeply. But after it opened and closed again, footsteps approached, and when a pale shape lurked on the other side of the frosted doors, Olivia panicked until, with a *thwap*, a second towel, white (the color of lilies), was flung over the top of the stall.

After her eventual exit from the bathroom, she slipped back into the clothes of a sensible, safe traveler, laced on her battered sneakers, and wiggled into her extra sweater, though she knew it would soon be tied around her waist in the trademark style of tourists and five year olds. She girded herself with a spacious water bottle and divided her cash among several pockets. There was a rhythm to these things Miranda had taught her to do.

She even ate breakfast, though it was awkward, because Miranda insisted on snatching the blow dryer from the bathroom and plugging it into a socket in the common room, wielding it against her sister while Olivia ate. Toast crumbs were dashed away into obscure corners, to be discovered some loveless day in the future when the building came down in ruins.

Marc, meanwhile, sat sedately on one of the couches, listening to Lenny describe Lima to him after having asked him what it was like.

"Lenny works for the magazine *Lonely Planisphere*," Miranda said as she tugged away at Olivia's hair with a wide-toothed, but still unforgiving, comb. "She knows exactly how to visit places. It's her job."

"What does she do on her vacations?" Olivia asked. "Stay at home?"

"Lenny is a very experienced traveler," Miranda said. "You should listen to what she says. Except when she invites you to do something unsafe. Did you use conditioner?"

"I couldn't take it with me on the plane."

"Well, at least you don't have to wash this pile every day. Put it up and no one will notice what a mess it is."

Olivia did so obediently, fingers finding their places on the back of her head. She concentrated fiercely on mentally cataloguing all she knew about Gaudí, and was so absorbed that they reached the bottom step, and were out the door before she even thought to ask what they'd see first.

"We'll start far and work our way in," Lenny said. "It saves time and you feel more energized by the end. That was in my first column. So we'll hit the Sagrada Familia, then head to the Casa Milá, and end on the Casa Batlló, since it's right around the corner."

"If you don't mind, I might stay behind to visit some of the museums inside," Marc said. "But if it holds you back, you can go ahead without me."

"Oh, we'll be visiting the museums too," Lenny said. "We'll have time for everything."

They turned left and headed north into Barcelona's calm, orderly nineteenth-century district. Olivia thought it was pacific, to be swept along with others' plans.

They marched along in unacknowledged and uncomfortable silence until it became gradually evident that, in a city sector renowned for its orderly grid, they had managed to lose their way. It wasn't really a surprise, considering that the more they pretended to be watching for important turns, the less attention they were actually paying to anything they saw.

Miranda pulled out a map. "Oh no," Lenny said, snatching it away. "How do you think you're ever going to learn a city if you're always resorting to a map? You have to wander a little. You have to get lost! You drift until you find your way again."

They chewed on this for another half hour until Marc unobtrusively pulled his own map out of his pocket and, unfolding it inconspicuously, pinpointed the Sagrada Familia, and then their current location, and— most impressive of all—connected the two with an easily discernable route. Even Lenny couldn't argue with that logic, especially because she was also adhering to her rule of never stopping at a café until her destination was in sight, and breakfast was wearing off a little.

But past the orderly blocks of homes with shops built into the bottoms, past the large buildings cut clean with precise filigree details and bulging iron balconies, and past the color patterns of flowers and women, delicate and regular as if they were papered on the outside, the spires rose. If yesterday's cathedral had melted and stretched itself more gelatinously toward the sky, Olivia would have been looking at these towers instead, and she would not have been in the Gothic Quarter at all, and the accordion player would have played without her.

Antoni Gaudí's buildings were Art Nouveau, constructed in the late nineteenth and early twentieth centuries. Many of his most famous works were scattered throughout Barcelona. They resembled not homes and churches, but sandcastles brought to full size and mosaics taken to the third dimension. Olivia knew this from all she'd read the evening before, and as they gazed upon the towering work of art, Olivia saw it was true. Lenny ran into the nearby gas station for a sandwich, and Miranda followed to use the bathroom. Marc tried to make the case that they might as well get an early lunch, but Lenny insisted that food in any area near a major tourist site was embarrassingly overpriced. "Only tourists eat near a tourist attraction," she said.

On the second approach, they entered the church, and everyone, including Lenny, handed over seven grudging euro to explore Gaudí's unfinished temple. Construction of the Temple Expiatori de la Sagrada Familia had begun in 1882, and it was still being built today, over a hundred years later, funded entirely by donations and alms. Twelve bell towers, a soaring interior, and eye-numbingly complex façades of unique sculpture were all molded into Gaudí's surreal, oozing style. Tourists were allowed into certain mostly complete sections of the church, but its wide-open interior allowed glimpses of the ongoing work as well.

Olivia stood under the contorted, fibrous, yawning stone mouth of the main door, newer by construction but older by design than the dense clockwork of the gothic cathedral. It was primordial, gaping, almost horrifying in its thick-set power. It reminded her of the monsters in her books, and she felt the heroes' fear—an empathy that had faded long ago once she'd learned the end of every adventure.

"Come on," Miranda said in her ear. "We don't have time to stand around. Let's go inside."

After taking the same picture on three cameras, they walked inside, into a forest only Olivia could see. Among the solemn oaks of the Cathedral of Barcelona, she had felt like a girl among ancient monoliths. Here she felt like an ant or a beetle buried deep between the stalks of fertile lotuses. Unfinished as the church was, the scaffolding which filled it became a part of the artwork and caught the colored light of two stained-glass windows—red, blue, green—like spider webs at dawn. The spiders, in bright yellow reflective vests, climbed up and down them.

Marc thought of the streets where he had grown up, the yawning buildings a giant mouth penning him in, tendons stretching to swallow him whole, and rendering the sky insignificant. He had had terrible claustrophobia as a child. Sometimes his bedroom seemed too small, like a shoe that would never fit.

Now, in the cavernous church, he didn't see the vast spaces—only the walls. He thought about the things his mother had done to help him escape his fears—games of imagining he was somewhere else, games of imagining he was some*one* else, some little boy who wasn't afraid.

Lenny saw a sea cave she had once visited with a local guide in Greece. There with three other travelers, she was the last to scramble out of the boat and onto a ledge to explore. As the guide reached up to help her out, his hand slid lower down her back.

He was old, with chipped yellow teeth that framed the holes in his smile. She felt a wave of disgust, and suddenly wished she were home, back in the house her parents had finally bought in Colorado after she'd gone away to college, once her dad had retired. It was the first time she had realized she couldn't remember what the bookshelves in her Chicago apartment looked like, or the other houses on the street where her family had lived when she was in middle school.

But the moment had been fleeting. At every new sight, the other tourists loved asking her what it was like to be a travel writer, so Lenny had no choice but to be one.

Miranda didn't see much at all. She didn't really like modern architecture.

As they skirted the interior, looking up silently and separately, their imaginations moved to complete its construction. They passed right by the large signs describing the building's history.

Without conversing, they planted themselves neatly at the end of the line for visiting the roof. There was only one elevator, which took tourists up to the top of a bell tower with a spectacular view.

"The sign says the wait is an hour," Olivia said quietly to her sister.

"But it's on the list," Miranda said. "I think you'd regret not going. The guidebook says it's one of the best ways to see the whole city."

Olivia recalled the Cathedral roof and Greg, and her conversation with Mr. Brown.

"Okay," she murmured. "Sounds nice."

She stood by her sister's elbow for a few more minutes before she tapped Miranda's shoulder again and said, "Can you hold my place in line? I want to look around some more."

"If you don't mind, I think I'll go with her," Marc said, smiling.

Olivia was a little disappointed, but she thought there was a better chance of shaking Marc than Lenny or Miranda. In fact, she suspected Marc just wanted to get away from them, too.

Sure enough, they parted immediately, each exiting the church a different way. Olivia let her gaze drift, sipping slowly what she had gulped in before. She felt a slight tension, as if she were looking for something.

While she took in the beauty and variety of the church, the image of Miranda waiting in line rose in Olivia's mind. Olivia wished Miranda would enjoy herself more. Miranda hadn't seemed to enjoy anything wholeheartedly for years now.

There had been a time when Miranda had seemed open. When she was in high school and Olivia in elementary school, she used to curl up on Olivia's bed and tell her about boys who had looked at her in the hall. She used to make social life, grown-up life, sound like stories of adventure like the ones Olivia loved to read. One night, flouncing home from a high school dance, she crept into Olivia's bedroom, knowing she'd find Olivia up past her bedtime reading with a flashlight, and took the book out of Olivia's hands and told her to live a little.

Now, Miranda was the stern chaperone, and Olivia was afraid it was because she, like everyone else, was expected to eventually grow out of affection and excitement.

After a little time spent looking around and following their own thoughts, Olivia and Marc managed to wander back to the same façade, smiling first, then drifting closer until they were simply waiting for the other to break the silence.

Marc sat down on a balustrade and crossed his legs, waiting for Olivia to join him, which she did, sheepishly.

"Aren't the pictures stories?" she asked, pointing lazily up at the rippling façade, from which rounded faces and supplicant bodies emerged in a chaotic tangle. "Do you know what any of them are?"

"I can't tell," he said, then cleared his throat. "Some of them look less than pleasant."

Olivia turned and looked at the street beyond the church.

"There's a park there," she said. "With palm trees. And a green pond. The paths are made of dirt."

Marc turned and looked as well.

"Look, they've got some Scottish people there, too," he said, pointing out the cluster of blue jerseys. "I was trying to look this up. Are the palm trees indigenous to this area, or do you think they just planted them there to make the city more beachy and tropical?"

"They look perfect in that park," Olivia said. "I think I just saw a green bird flying away from there."

"Probably the sheen on a pigeon. Though maybe, when they brought the palm trees, they also brought tropical birds."

"Maybe it escaped from one of the street stalls," Olivia said.

"A satisfactory conclusion. I couldn't have put it better myself." Marc laughed. "Thank you for saving me from my own cynicism."

Olivia smiled.

"Do you and your sister travel together a lot?" Marc asked.

"This is my first time out of the U.S., actually. She's done more. She's already been to—"

"Madrid. She told me."

Olivia laughed.

"Well," she said, "I deferred my freshman year of college, and I—I wasn't doing much of anything, and Miranda said I should go out and get some culture. I think she sees it more like a super-concentrated pre-college study abroad than a vacation."

Olivia sighed. She had felt the strain of Miranda's expectations, especially because Miranda had paid for her own half of the trip herself, while their mother was paying for Olivia, pocket money and all. Olivia felt she owed it to them both to make an effort to learn and be grown-up.

"Do you have any other siblings?"

"No." She paused uncomfortably when she realized she was on the verge of saying they barely had a mother.

Olivia's silence terminated the conversation. They turned together to look again at the incomplete church.

"How long has it been?" Olivia asked when it seemed to be long enough.

"We can go in and see where they are," Marc said.

Lenny and Miranda weren't far from where they had been before, but several noisy families had accumulated behind them in line, so at least they felt they'd made some progress. As Marc and Olivia slid up the winding maze of the rope barriers, the noisy families escalated their volume, and a few of the more alert children wailed. Apparently, it was unfair to cut in such a slow line, even if someone had been legitimately holding a place for them.

Marc and Olivia decided to retreat, agreeing to meet Lenny and Miranda outside, near the entrance where they'd all come in.

Together, Olivia and Marc drifted down the undulating steps of the church and out into the street. There were souvenir shops to be examined and the park to explore—but not, it turned out, to linger in. For in addition to palm trees and green pigeons, it was home to the rich scent of sewage, which began with the public water closets dominating the far corner.

After walking until they were hollow with hunger and footsore enough to mar anything new they might see, Olivia and Marc agreed to break Lenny's rule and get food. They searched until they found the perfect café—that is, the one exactly like every other café they had passed, and within easy sight of the agreed-upon meeting point, that being the booth where they had first entered the Sagrada Familia. The café was a cross between a coffee shop and a diner, with vinyl-padded seats, shiny black and white tiles, and an exotic menu. While they waited for their food, they watched, mildly bemused, as the waiters gently deflected wandering beggars from the outdoor seating.

A man with a clarinet and another on tenor sax set up by the bench on the other side of the pavement, and Olivia and Marc sat back to watch the scene for another hour. Their growing concern for the others was offset by their growing irritation and boredom. What had started as light chattiness ran dry and lapsed into companionable silence, but even that began to sour as the wait grew longer.

At last, Lenny and Miranda emerged from the church courtyard and swayed toward their waiting friends. After getting to the top, Lenny had suggested they take the spiral stairs down the spire so they wouldn't have to pay the elevator fee again. (To prevent congestion on the narrow stairs, the church's managers forbade tourists from climbing *up* them.) Besides, they'd get to look through all the little windows on the way. Miranda, whose vertigo had practically overwhelmed her at the top, stopped on every landing to close her eyes.

They were ready for lunch, overpriced or not, and they didn't mind that Olivia and Marc would have to wait a while longer. Miranda sat next to her sister and, sensing her restlessness, squeezed her hand under the table. It grounded her. Soon, Olivia discovered a fresh wave of hunger in time to join in on their greasy, messy, chattering meal.

After another hour, they set off, having crossed out the museum at the top of the Casa Milá due to the loss of time at the Sagrada Familia, which Marc had anticipated all along. They stayed just long enough at Milá to snap a dozen digital pictures, but from the street level, the complex looked a bit bland and malformed—"like a gray plastic house left in front of a radiator," according to Marc, and they all agreed. They moved on to the Casa Batlló.

The Casa Battló was just around the corner from their hostel. Olivia's guidebooks told her that the embellishments of the building, with its vertebrae balconies and scaled roof, depicted St. George defeating the dragon. Olivia looked forward to finding the story in its molten folds.

Olivia remembered playing with Miranda in the backyard when she was very, very small, sitting on the lowest branches of the tree they called a tower and pretending the neighbor's dog was a dragon. While Miranda, who always insisted on being the queen, shouted orders to an imaginary army of knights below, never waiting to be saved, Olivia, the princess, had thought how nice it would be to languish, as long as she had a steady supply of books and food. Miranda would tease her for it, then dare her to run into the neighbor's yard.

(When Olivia had told their mother about the games, their mother had said something cryptic about eating up the patriarchal myths of the Romantic era and told her to instead pretend to be an archeologist leading her own expedition.)

So Olivia had looked forward to the Casa Battló, but by the time they arrived, their visit was limited to a neck-snapping stare at the exterior, thanks to impossibly long lines and an early closing hour.

They tried to enjoy that for a while, crossed the street to see if they could catch a glimpse of the tiled roof from that angle (they couldn't), and then ducked in front of people who had just finished taking a picture and walked blindly in front of those who were just about to.

"And that's how you do Gaudí in a day," Lenny croaked triumphantly as they shuffled toward Casa Joven, each person uniquely disappointed.

"Now we know," Marc said.

Olivia remembered seeing water from the top of the Cathedral of Barcelona yesterday. She remembered the streaming air up there, and the transformation that had occurred below while she'd waited, floating, above. Reaching for Miranda's hand, she said, "Let's go to the beach. I haven't seen the beach yet."

"It's been a long day," Miranda said, extricating her hand. She was afraid of Olivia's tone, which had the desperate excitement that had preceded her dives into fantastic waking dreams.

"But you can't say you've been to Barcelona without seeing the Mediterranean," Lenny said. "I could use a good drink in a beach bar somewhere."

"It's only a few stops away," Marc said. "We can take the Metro."

"Well." Miranda sighed. The enthusiasm of the others eased her concern. "I like listening to the waves. It could be relaxing. And it shouldn't be too crowded in the off-season."

They walked past their hostel and down a few more blocks to the Plaça

Catalunya Metro, where they were swallowed by its bareness and the hot scent of metal and oil. A guitarist in the tile-paved tunnel played songs by the Police.

"I only give them change if they sing in Spanish," Lenny said, the only comment made as they waited on the platform.

The ride of five stops was agonizing, and so was the strenuous walk from the closest stop to the beach, toward the twin high-rises that towered over the sand. Perplexing curvaceous artwork and blocky hotels shot up around them, crested, and ebbed away, and Olivia broke into a jog, charged with a childlike impatience, until she was stopped by the pavement railing that overlooked the beach and the sea.

She waited there until the others caught up, but as soon as they did, Olivia dashed off again, down along the rail and past an advertisement asking swimmers if they were thirsty, and tripped down the slide of sandy dirt and stringy grass to the beach, warm, glowing, and alive.

A green bird flew from a tree.

The water was blue and white.

The air smelled like fish.

Black and brown rocks neatly cut the coast into groomed partitions.

A thickset woman in a forest-green bikini sunned herself on the sand, alone, while passing walkers laughed at her or pretended to ignore her.

Olivia threw herself down the beach, gathering up with swaying arms every gift thrown to her—like the wind that blew off the water and made her clothing mold against her body, shift, and cling again, and made her cheeks bright and her eyes fill. She felt the sea throwing swells toward her that billowed and fell and grew again to crash as waves and cast out shy, quiet, shallow washes, eaten again by the following waves. She stumbled out of her shoes, leaving them somewhere upside-down behind her on the sand.

She felt the water beating against her hips, under her feet, under the palms of her hands, encircling her waist, sliding down the taut muscles of her legs, smoothing over the curves of her waving arms. It created something: a solid body that arose from the waves, panting and smiling, alive. He rolled toward her, legs awash, dripping with the many rivulets that composed his body, blue and white, green and brown and black. The sun struck him and made him real.

"Olivia! Olivia!" he yelled. The form that had emerged from the waves was Greg Brown.

"Olivia! I will wade out!" Wade out? He was already out. He spoke too soon; the sea tossed another wave up at him and knocked at his knees, and he fell into the water, dissolving and resolving, standing, laughing, his mouth full of laughter, while she crept slowly into the water toward him.

"Olivia! I will wade out, 'til my thighs are steeped in burning flowers!" he called to her. He emerged again from the water after another dunk. "I will take the sun in my mouth."

Now, his feet encrusted with sand and water streaming down his slicked masses of hair, his eyes were filled with the sea and the sun and with her. He leaned toward her. His smiling mouth spoke.

"I waded out, 'til my thighs were steeped in burning flowers. I took the sun in my mouth, and I leaped into the ripe air."

Alive, the sea answered. *With closed eyes.*

To dash against darkness, the green bird said.

In the sleeping curves of my body, Olivia's skin sang.

Her mouth was smiling without her permission. Her throat was laughing without her awareness. Her eyes were streaming with the sea blown into them.

He stepped quickly forward and his mouth covered hers, and t was salt and the taste of his skin and the waves that danced around their ankles and an overwhelming warmth.

They had no names.

Olivia?

"Olivia!"

"Olivia!" Miranda repeated. Miranda, coming down the beach, first saw two figures against the blinding water, and then—then, she saw her sister clasped by someone who—attacked? No, kissing—Greg Brown. She wished she could somehow take the Browns' private room and throw it back in their faces.

She wanted to make it hurt.

"Olivia, get back here!" Olivia heard her sister's voice over the deafening cry of the sea. With the awkwardness of being seen kissing by her sister, she pulled away and ran back.

"Where are your shoes?" Miranda snapped. Olivia found them, picked them up, dusted her feet, and put them on. She trembled. A pillar stood on the edge of the water—Greg, standing in the waves, smiling. She stood looking at him, and the warmth flowed back, until Miranda pulled on her arm and they walked back up the beach and onto the concrete.

The back of her shirt was still damp, like the print of his dripping hand.

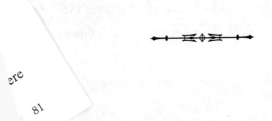

Miranda hoped Lenny and Marc hadn't seen. As it turned out, they had been busy hiding their dislike for each other (his mild, hers intense) by chattering nonstop, and most of their remarks had been directed at the soaring bronze sculpture down the boardwalk, which he thought looked like a whale, and she thought looked like a helmet. When Miranda trudged up, they were both looking in the direction opposite of where Olivia and Greg had been.

"Are you guys coming to the beach bar with us?" Lenny asked.

"No. Olivia's tired and we're going back," Miranda said.

"In that case, I'll join you," Marc said.

"I'll just make some new friends at the bar," Lenny said, chuckling artificially as she meandered away in the opposite direction.

Olivia looked back down onto the beach, where the orange and red were fading into deep juniper blue, an ink stain across the sky. She saw someone dive into the water, submerge, and float back up. He was swimming. He had swallowed the sun, and he would wait in the water and glide through it until he could set his teeth in the silver of the moon.

6

SHE RISES SHE

Olivia, Miranda, and Marc roared through Barcelona's underground. Emerging again to the street, they found the darkness had followed them up. After a gentle uphill walk of ten minutes past street stalls and lost-looking tourists, they came upon the hidden little entry of Casa Joven, climbed the stairs, and tumbled through the big green door, Marc breaking off to go to the dorm room.

"We're going to have a long talk after you get out of there," Miranda said as Olivia stepped into the bathroom. "I'll be waiting."

Olivia chose between two showers. She opened the one that had been hers this morning and, turning the free handle on her feet only, washed away the last grains of sand. With wet feet, she padded to the mirror and looked at herself. Her hair had escaped in tendrils from her bun, rising in a wild halo around her head. Her eyes were large and nervous. She sighed and looked at her parted lips. They were freshly red. They were—

"That's it!" Miranda said, walking in and shutting the door behind her. "What the hell just happened out there?"

"I don't know."

"Don't try that with me."

"Let me out. Miranda, I want to go back to our room," said Olivia. "This is weird. What if someone wants to come in here?"

"I'm not letting you out until you talk to me," Miranda said, placing herself in front of the door. "I saw you and Greg."

"I know," Olivia said with a groan. Unconsciously, she raised a hand and touched her mouth.

"What was that all about?" Miranda asked, sounding, to Olivia's surprise, a little diminished. "I thought this week was supposed to be about us. A sister week."

"I know," Olivia whispered. She wanted to add, "It was just a kiss," but it wasn't.

"And I feel like you've been ignoring me," Miranda said. "Yesterday you left me all alone, and then you came back with that kid. And today you left me behind to be with him again. And you didn't even tell me you two had a . . . thing."

"I'm sorry," Olivia said, her voice becoming very small. She wanted to say, "We don't have a thing," but that didn't seem right, either.

"I didn't think you were like that. Not that you've done anything wrong," Miranda said, gaining some strength in her voice again as Olivia blushed. "But we've only been here two days, and I didn't think you were the kind who went for vacation flings."

"I don't know," Olivia said. She felt as if a rock was sitting in her throat. Her lips trembled. She remembered the times when her sister used to talk about encountering boys as if it were the most interesting thing a person could do. That Miranda had disappeared some time ago. "I thought you said I didn't do anything wrong."

Miranda relaxed against the bathroom door. "No, you're okay," she said. "I just thought we'd get more time together than this." She hitched up a sorry smile that was half condescending and half conspiratorial. "And you don't want Greg. Take him out of Barcelona and he's a total hick."

The words were unexpectedly harsh, especially in the forced nonchalance with which they were delivered. Olivia had never had a boyfriend, and she knew Miranda knew that.

Olivia wondered if it was possible to explain the roof of the Cathedral. The way Mr. Brown's smile had smoothed away her anxiety. The way the church had looked different when she came down again. How she had felt alive. And the story of the accordion player and her lost mask and eating pretzels with Greg in the crowded plaza. The feeling of Greg's hand around her own.

"I thought he liked me," Olivia said softly.

"And what isn't there to like?" Miranda said, pulling her into a hug. "That's why I want to make sure no one walks over you. You deserve better."

They rocked in straining silence for a few moments.

"Hey, Miranda," Olivia murmured, "please don't tell Mom." Olivia didn't know what made her more nervous—her mother's political outrage that she would waste her time wrapping herself up with some stupid male, or just the simple embarrassment of being caught.

Miranda pulled back slightly.

"Why would I?" Miranda said. "It'll be our sister secret."

"Okay. Thanks."

"Hey, I'm here for you, kiddo. And I'm not going anywhere," Miranda said. "Quick nap and then dinner?"

"Okay," Olivia said.

"You're tired. We'll just take it easy tonight."

"Okay."

Miranda slipped out the door and shut it again behind her, leaving Olivia alone.

Olivia stepped to the sink, wet her face, and dried it carefully with a white towel. She let down her hair, combed it half-heartedly, and tied it up again. She looked in the mirror. She was clean, orderly. But even the smallest of motions sent shivers over her body. For a long time, she had hid a very deep well of affection, desperate to pulley it up in buckets and pour it over someone.

She'd once looked to her sister and her mother, but been afraid the water would have beaded and rolled right off their backs, so she'd saved it for her books and private thoughts. She often imagined that, if she'd had a chance to meet and get to know her father, she could have given a large portion of her affection to him, and when she'd heard he was dead, it was like the passing of an opportunity more than the passing of a person.

But this was different. She sensed she had connected with someone who would receive her downpour with joy, dance in it, and invite her to dance with him.

She hoped that sleep would wash her confusion away—sleep and clean socks. And, she hoped, a healthy, filling dinner in a warm, quiet restaurant far away from tourists and Scottish football fans would ease Miranda's fears. She hoped she could sneak through the rest of her vacation without running into or even seeing Greg Brown again, or she might die, or combust with embarrassment, or hurt her sister—or she might kiss him again, softly, his lips between her lips, and hear the sea that followed him into even the quietest room.

Olivia was surprised by how exhausted she was when she finally laid herself down on her bed. She dropped off quickly into a flat, blank sleep so heavy that when she awoke again, she wasn't sure she'd slept at all. At first, she was overwhelmed with the sensation that she was in her bed at home, that it was spring, and that the dogwoods were tapping her window with brightness, and everything was turned around. But the feeling just came from the smell of the old sweatshirt she had rested her head upon.

As she read one of her guidebooks, Miranda sat tensely in the common room, telling herself she wasn't waiting for Greg to return. Miranda wondered again what the private room had really cost. She kept expecting the Browns to exact some kind of tribute for their supposed good deed. But underneath that, she was afraid they really were as nice as they seemed.

Olivia dozed serenely in that private room, behind the closed door, the translucent curtains pulled, and Miranda waited, thinking she was waiting for her sister to wake up. She waited so intently that Marc gave up on trying to gain her attention and wandered off to speak Spanglish with Hugo in the kitchen, the tall, lean adult and the short, compact young man mumbling awkwardly out of Miranda's earshot, but just close enough to irritate her as she pretended to focus on the open page.

At last, in the November crispness that follows a warm day, Greg gusted in, coat pulled lazily over his damp shirt, his hair matted with sun and water. His stride was loose and relaxed, and though he didn't quite smile, he tunelessly hummed some song he must have heard in his head. These things made Miranda furious, especially because they were new on Greg, and she knew immediately they were because he had kissed her sister.

As Greg left the room, she instead glared at Hugo and Marc in the kitchen, but they were talking and didn't notice her, so she got up and followed Greg into the dormitory room. It was empty except for the two of them, and there he was, toweling his hair vigorously at the end of the room near the window where Miranda and her sister were supposed to be, a new shirt hanging off his shoulders. He turned, and his grin faded in the face of Miranda's taut frown.

"I want to talk to you," she said.

Greg came toward her into the darkness of the room and stood dimly, leaning against the bunk nearest where she stood, her hand still on the knob of the door. She took a step backwards.

"I don't know what you're trying to do with my sister," she said, "but it has to stop."

Greg opened his mouth, but no sound came out.

"She's in a very fragile place right now, and I won't have you making it worse," Miranda said.

"I don't understand," Greg murmured.

"Just—don't—just leave her alone, okay?" Miranda said, losing her train of thought. Anyway, she owed him no explanations about Olivia.

Greg continued to look clueless.

"Did I do something wrong?" he asked, earnestly.

Miranda couldn't squeeze a word out of her throat for a dumbfounded second.

"Yes!" she exploded at last. "Of course! You—you took advantage of her!"

Greg's face faded into the dusky twilight of the room. He stepped backwards into the darkness, silhouetted against the blue glow of the curtains, and Miranda couldn't see his mouth as he said, "I'm sorry. I didn't realize."

His tone was terrifying in its softness. It wasn't as Miranda had imagined. She'd done what she believed was best to protect her little sister, and instead she had hurt this stupid boy who somehow insisted on seeming nice. Miranda felt propelled from the room.

On her way back down the hall, she crashed into Marc.

"What's going on?" he said, laughing. "Were you and Greg having some private time?"

Miranda was incapable of responding.

"Hold it," he said, whirling around just as they passed each other and catching up to her again. "I wanted to talk to you. Hugo gave me an idea for something we could do tomorrow."

"Let me brush your hair first," Miranda said. "It got all thatchy while you slept on it."

Olivia scooted to the edge of the bed and leaned her head forward so her sister could tidy her hair, as if it weren't a part of her but a nuisance to be objectively eliminated. Miranda slipped behind her on the bed and took the thick tangles in her hands, folded them into a neat roll, and secured it on the back of Olivia's head with a vast multitude of bobby pins.

"You look very sophisticated with your hair up like that," Miranda said. "You look almost twenty."

"I *am* almost twenty," Olivia said.

Miranda just hugged her awkwardly from behind and climbed down again to sort out her purse.

"Come on, I'll treat you," Miranda said.

They walked to a restaurant on La Rambla located between several noisy sports bars. They read their menus and ordered. Silence spoke from Olivia's hooded eyes and sealed mouth.

The glass-shaded lamps of the restaurant glowed green, and the square white plates contrasted with the smallness of the pieces of bread rubbed with tomato. The hum of other diners only emphasized their own silence. Miranda could barely swallow, but Olivia discovered an appetite, and as she ate, her mouth working over the textures and flavors of a wide variety of small items, her voice dislodged itself from its hiding place.

"What are we going to do tomorrow?" Olivia asked with plastic curiosity. "I want to do some real exploring."

Miranda chewed and swallowed and stared.

"Marc wants to hike up Montjuic," she said. "Well, it's not an actual hike. It's really just a sidewalk with some trees. But there's a garden museum. Or a castle. Or something."

"Sounds like fun. I'll read about it tonight," Olivia said. "Do you think there's a place still open tonight where we can get a few more books?

I want to make sure I really enjoy it this time. Not that I haven't been having fun."

Miranda was happy that Olivia sounded a bit more alive, but there was an edge to her sudden interest that scared her a little bit. So she didn't respond. Forks clicked. Plates were set. Glasses filled. The scent of roasted peppers, toasted bread, olive oil, and shellfish rose.

"Where do you think Lenny is?" Olivia asked.

"I don't know," Miranda said. "Sometimes, I don't want to know."

"You know, I don't think I'd really like her if I met her back home," Olivia said as she cracked open a crayfish. "But she is kind of entertaining."

"Yeah. She can tell a good story," Miranda said, searching her mind for a single example as soon as the words were out of her mouth.

"You think so?" Olivia said. "I mean, travel stories are weird. All the feeling gets lost in the details. I wonder if she's any good."

"At what?"

"As a writer," said Olivia. "I mean, she's got to be, if she works for *Lonely Planisphere*. But I've never actually read it."

"Don't be a gossip," Miranda said.

A group seated nearby erupted in laughter at some private joke.

Olivia leaned forward with a new light in her eyes.

"You'll make sure everything's okay tomorrow, right?" she said.

"Of course," Miranda said, unsure what she meant. She reached for her sister's hand to squeeze it, but Olivia had hid it under the table, tangling it in the napkin on her lap.

"I'm bothering you," Olivia said.

"No! Not at all! What gave you that idea?" Miranda said.

"You went to all this trouble to convince Mom to let us go on this trip, and now I'm ruining it," Olivia said.

"Quit it," Miranda said. "I'm only here to make *you* feel better."

Olivia digested the idea slowly. They finished their dinner, paid the check, and slumped back to the hostel, where Lenny was nowhere to be seen. Hugo said he knew nothing of her whereabouts.

"I'm starting to get worried," Miranda said.

"I thought you said she's been here before," Olivia said. "She can take care of herself."

"Maybe Hugo didn't understand the question," Miranda said, choosing to forget that Hugo was only ignorant of English when Miranda spoke it.

Miranda was relieved no one had been around to see them slink back in so miserably, but the relief was short-lived. She heard the outer door open and close while she and Olivia were in the bathroom, brushing their teeth too thoroughly.

Peeking out with her toothbrush handle still sticking out from her cheek, Miranda saw down the hall that Mr. Brown and the Polish couple were finally back from another dinner together. Greg had emerged from the dorm room as well, and they were all in the common room, speaking with Hugo with irritating cheerfulness.

Olivia noticed her sister acting strangely and asked what was wrong. Miranda gestured to the sight down the hall, then drew Olivia back quickly and shut the door again. There was a little thrill in acting secretively that Miranda couldn't resist.

"If we go quickly, they might not even notice us," Miranda whispered.

"They aren't even looking in our direction," Olivia said, though she couldn't help whispering in return.

"Come on, let's go," Miranda said, and they ran out. It was only a few steps from the bathroom to their bedroom, but Olivia couldn't stop herself from staring down the hall at the crowd they were trying to avoid.

That instant, Greg looked in their direction and their eyes met briefly before she was pulled into the bedroom and Miranda shut the door.

"That was close!" Miranda exclaimed, then laughed shrilly. Olivia didn't see what was funny.

"Are you going to read, or can I turn out the light?" Olivia asked, climbing under her blanket.

Miranda's nervous excitement was doused by Olivia's tone. Her face fell, and she couldn't respond.

"I'm going to turn out the light, then," Olivia said, irritation in her voice, and she pulled the string, leaving Miranda to shuffle to her bed in darkness. Once Miranda was secure in her bed, the blankets pulled up around her neck, she realized she absolutely could not sleep, but had a vague suspicion she'd rather cry instead. It was the first night since arriving that she had gone to bed not worrying about Olivia's mental state. Olivia explained part of her anxiety, but Miranda realized a larger part of it had to do with herself.

Miranda never remembered her dreams. When she woke up at four in the morning with a dry mouth, she had the dim impression of dogwood trees in blurs of color and sound, which vanished quickly in the pressing darkness, shaken out by a crash she hadn't heard consciously but was loud enough to wake her. She tried to sleep again but couldn't, and instead lay in bed with her eyes closed, waiting for her travel alarm clock to wake Olivia.

7

SO TIMID AIR IS FIRM

Lenny had slipped in around four that morning. During an otherwise graceful dance to her bed, she had crashed into the doorframe of her room. Lenny herself was the reason she always told travelers to bring earplugs and eyeshades to a hostel.

Later that morning, too early according to her pounding skull (but not soon enough according to her churning stomach), Lenny sat at the kitchen table with her head in her hands.

"Oh God, kill me now," she said with a moan. She groped for a partially filled water bottle she'd brought in with her and took a grimacing sip of its chartreuse contents.

"Everything okay?" Miranda croaked as she wandered into the common room.

"Mugh," Lenny said.

"Do you need anything?" Miranda asked, putting on a pot of coffee.

"A multivitamin," Lenny said.

Miranda stopped, holding the water-filled carafe in the air.

"Really?" she asked.

"Best hangover remedy I know," Lenny said. "To replenish the body and wash out the bad stuff."

Miranda wanted to say something like, "Why do you have to show off how smart you are even when you do something stupid?" but it came out as, "Sorry, I don't have any."

Miranda did make a point to travel with a broad selection of headache and stomach medicines, but she wasn't sure how many of anything Lenny had already taken, and she also wasn't sure whether she wanted to know. She did the best she figured she could, returning to Lenny's table with a tall glass of water and a piece of toast.

Lenny seemed compelled by Miranda's slightly disapproving lack of questions to explain what she had been doing the night before.

"Research," Lenny moaned, bypassing the water Miranda had set down for her sickly water bottle. "This is all in the name of research," she said, waving her free arm as if the empty common room were a part of her hangover.

"What is that?" Miranda asked, looking at the bottle.

"The second-best remedy for hangovers," Lenny said. "Leftovers."

Miranda huffed.

"Do you really think that's a good idea?" she said. "What exactly were you drinking?"

"I was checking out an absinthe bar," Lenny said, reviving a little and nibbling on the corner of the toast. "It's a big trend. Legally, they can't serve the old-fashioned kind with wormwood in it, so it isn't hallucinatory. But the kids love to pretend." She chuckled a little, then turned slightly green and stopped.

"That bottle is full of . . . absinthe?" Miranda asked slowly.

Lenny nodded.

"Wouldn't it, um, melt the plastic?" Miranda said. "You could get plastic poisoning. Or something."

That's when Marc breezed in, humming, already dressed for the day's expedition.

"Olivia looks very pretty in the window," he said. "Like a painting."

Olivia had quietly slipped by while Miranda had been busy in the kitchen. As Marc had said, she sat in the window at the back of the room, next to fading lilies set against a piercing morning sunlight, reading *A Wrinkle in Time*. Her concentration was intense.

A gray cloud fell over Miranda. Without anything being overtly wrong that morning, nothing felt quite right, either. Everyone at breakfast seemed absorbed in themselves. Lenny was nauseated; Marc, whistling to himself, wandered in and out of the room gathering his things for the day; and Olivia had slipped in without even saying "good morning."

Miranda sighed and left the room to sit by herself on her bed and reorganize her purse yet again.

The sunlight in the morning had a different quality than during any other part of the day. It was bright but cool and penetrating, and best suited to reveal imperfections. But its direct glare strongly illuminated only one side of Olivia's face. The other side was sheltered in darkness.

Marc hadn't overheard the argument in the bathroom yesterday, but because of their perfect coolness, he could tell there was something amiss between the sisters. He was troubled by it. If they were absorbed in their own little spat, Marc would become an awkward third wheel in their sibling drama.

Then again, they didn't seem like the kind of girls who would bicker in public. Relatively pleasant people, they were almost mature, and interesting enough to make up the difference.

"Hugo said you were going up a mountain," said Mr. Brown, walking into the room behind Greg. He plugged in the kettle.

"Yes, with Miranda and Olivia," he said. "We're going to have a picnic at the castle."

"I'm coming, too," Lenny wheezed, to Marc's surprise. Her face was on the table, pillowed by her arms. Marc had assumed she was unconscious.

"Greg and I want to see the castle," Mr. Brown said. "I think he wants to sit up there and imagine Don Quixote." In the kitchen, Greg groaned. Marc laughed. "Mind if we tag along?"

"I don't have a problem," Marc said. He was already wondering what the combination would produce.

Olivia had heard the Browns come in, but she'd kept her eyes on her book, succeeding only in pretending to read. But when she heard Marc invite them along, her eyes shot up to the main room, and a wave of heat rippled up to her cheeks. Greg was quiet as usual and slightly pale. As they always did, their eyes met briefly, but this time Greg was the first to break off. Two patches of red stung his cheeks, and he looked quickly at his father, then to the floor.

Mr. Brown appeared completely unaware of his son's embarrassment. Olivia knew instantly Greg hadn't told him.

Closing her book, Olivia padded out of the room, keeping her shoulder turned to the group and her head down. Greg hadn't told his father. She couldn't imagine not telling *someone*. It probably meant he didn't care as much as she'd thought.

She thought of the sensitivity she had instantly ascribed to him on hearing his mother was dead. Maybe she was wrong about him. Maybe things just happened to people, but didn't shape them. Or maybe he was just an insensitive jerk.

Or maybe she was the one who made everything a big deal, and he did this sort of thing all the time. She didn't want someone who did this sort of thing all the time. She didn't do this sort of thing all the time. As much as she hated the idea, which tore at her, she wondered if Miranda had somehow, and for all the wrong reasons, been right.

She wondered if she, herself, had been right back in August, when her natural response to change, to hurt, was to seal herself inside her shell and create a new impervious world inside. Looking back, that time seemed like a half-forgotten dream and, like vertigo, it gave her a brief rush of fear.

She slipped into their bedroom and shut the door.

Miranda, looking up at Olivia, was troubled by the look on her face— her eyes glowed fiercely.

"What's going on?" Miranda asked, getting more nervous the longer Olivia stood in silence.

"Greg and his dad are coming along," Olivia fumed.

Miranda blinked. It took a few seconds to sink in.

"Today?" she asked. "With us?"

"Yes. And yes," Olivia said.

"How did that happen?" Miranda asked, her heart pounding. She felt as if she was three feet tall, holding a broken vase, and the Browns were the grown-ups who had just walked in. Miranda felt a sudden urge to throw her hands up and cry, "I didn't do it!"

"I don't know," Olivia said. "Marc let them. Or they just invited themselves. I don't know how they do these things." Having blown off the worst of her frustration, Olivia collapsed onto her bed.

"It'll be okay," Miranda said.

"No, it won't," Olivia groaned. "I don't want to see him. I don't want to talk to him. I want to spend time with *you*. Like we said we would. You made me promise."

Miranda felt another stab of guilt at the tone with which her sister repeated the word "want," as if it were a chore, like cleaning the dishes.

"We'll still be there together," Miranda said. "You don't have to talk to him if you don't want to."

Olivia sat up and flashed a glare at Miranda, as if she were missing an important point.

"We can't do anything about it now anyway," Miranda said weakly.

"Yes we can. *You* can," Olivia said. Barely audible, she murmured, "You're supposed to."

"I can't get rid of them if they're already coming along," Miranda said.

"What about your friend Lenny?" Olivia said. "She doesn't like them."

"I'm not sure Lenny will make it today," Miranda said.

"She has to come—and then she'll get the Browns to leave!" Olivia said.

"No she won't. They like everyone," Miranda said.

Olivia stood up with a huff.

"Is this some sort of punishment?" she asked, more to the ceiling than her sister. In silence, she pulled her socks on and finished neatening up and packing her bag. From the hall came sounds of people walking back and forth, to and from the bathroom and the dorm room, as the rest of the hostel awoke and got ready for the day.

After zipping up her bag, Olivia cast her eye around the room, then slapped her leg sharply.

"I left my book in the common room," she said. "Just let me know when we're ready to go."

When Olivia had her hand on the door handle, Miranda stopped her and said, "I'm sorry."

"For what?" Olivia replied coldly. "You didn't do anything."

"Have you had anything to eat yet?" Miranda asked, forcing a smile.

"I'm not hungry," Olivia said, leaving Miranda alone in the room.

Before they left, Miranda crept out and stuffed a few muffins in her backpack for her sister. She wasn't sure when she'd be brave enough to suggest she eat them, but Miranda felt a little better knowing they were there.

Lenny, it turned out, bounced back quickly as soon as she realized the rest of the group was getting ready to leave without her. She was a little less conversational than usual, but a hangover was no fun without an audience.

Marc and the Browns sat on the couches, chatting about the weather while the girls assembled. They were like two teams preparing for a relay marathon, only the girls looked like theirs would be in a desert, for all the stuff Miranda and Olivia planned to lug along. Marc had already gone out to collect food, and the full picnic bag sat at his feet, its contents gradually squishing together and mingling scents.

Just late enough to be certain everyone else was ready, Olivia emerged from her corner to stand slightly behind Miranda. Without much conversation, they shuffled down the hall, and Hugo, who was leaning on the front desk talking to Sophie, waved cheerily as they marched out.

Miranda was struck by the idea that Hugo not only knew all along how things would turn out—that the Browns would find a way into the trip and Greg and Olivia would be thrown together again—but had engineered it that way. Her old resentment of him surged, and she was so intent on shutting the front door on his face that she didn't realize Sophie was on the other side, trying to pull the door open to get out. With a grunt of frustration, Miranda let go of the knob, and the blonde girl darted out and down the stairs ahead of them. As the door swung shut again, Miranda could have sworn she heard Hugo chuckling.

Lenny led the way down the stairs while Marc waited beside the landing for Miranda to join him. But Miranda, noticing that no one stood between her sister and Greg Brown, ignored Marc and grabbed Olivia's arm, creating a wall with their bodies so no one else could walk alongside them.

8

INTO THE WATERS I RODE

Greg Brown wasn't happy. He hadn't been for at least three years, give or take a few weeks—not since the silent hospital bed where he had sat beside her before the end. Gradually, the unhappiness became a habit. He put it on with his shirt in the morning, and like his shirt, it was so ordinary he didn't stop to think about it much once it was there.

Today was different. It didn't fit right. It was more uncomfortable, prickly.

When he thought of Miranda's face yesterday, her tone, the words she had used, his ordinary unhappiness collapsed into a seething new kind. What an idiot he'd been. He must have embarrassed Olivia and her sister and himself, and probably his father, too. He had just wanted to act like the poems, but maybe he had been selfish. Miranda certainly made it sound that way. And Olivia hadn't said anything at all.

On the walk to the Metro, he hung behind his father, afraid to approach anyone, the Somersets especially. But through the chaotic shuffle onto the Metro train, packed in with a crowd of tourists who didn't pay attention to where they or their elbows were going, Greg was forced in next to Miranda. He clung grimly and silently to a ceiling strap the entire ride, and when they changed trains to a different line, he held firm, like a rock against the tide of onrushing travelers, until he was certain he would board well after Miranda, with a buffer of several strangers between them.

As he emerged from the clinging darkness of the Metro and looked up at the double pillars of the Plaça d'Espanya, Greg Brown stood apart from the rest of the group. The Metro had brought them to the very bottom of the little mountain.

Mr. Brown soon joined his son and smiled up at the sun.

"Look at the way the light makes them look even bigger," he said of the pillars. "But I wonder why they put them there. They don't seem to be doing anything, or decorating anything."

Lenny had not taken off her sunglasses since leaving the hostel, but she was unprepared for the brightness outside.

"It's fucking bright out today," she growled to Marc on the escalator out of the Metro.

"Technically, I think we *are* marginally closer to the sun," Marc said smoothly.

Miranda and Olivia arrived next. They didn't speak at all. Though their arms were no longer locked, they stood close enough to discourage outside conversation.

Olivia squinted and could barely see.

Her guidebooks had told her that the Plaça d'Espanya, where they stood now, was one of the largest squares in Barcelona; that, like the Plaça Catalunya, it was the meeting of several major arteries of the city; and that the two Venetian towers they looked up at now, hulking square pillars with pyramid tops, pointed the way up the mountain. Past the towers, two flights of steps flanked a sloping park. Above, the steps emptied onto a wide, sunny terrace, and from there a final flight of steps, like the ones in the front of important civic buildings back home, led up to a gleaming palace, rounded and sprawling. They were looking up at Montjuic, the lonely mountain that peered over Barcelona and its port.

As Miranda shaded her eyes, her first thought was of the vertigo the tower builders must have felt at the base of the climb. Disoriented, she looked down again.

They marched up the slanting ground.

"It looks like the Magic Fountain is under repair," Marc said, referring to the famous centerpiece fountains on the terraces between the stairs. "Too bad." Instead of tiers of dancing water, there were only empty concrete pools in the center of each wide landing that led to a hulking, ornate building presiding over what appeared, from that angle, to be the top of the mountain. The only working segment of the Magic Fountain was up there, a faint mist in the distance right in front of the Palau. Surreally, a pragmatic-looking escalator like the one they had just taken out of the Metro ran alongside the stone steps up the mountain. Although most of the tourists were ascending that way, the group eyed the stairs.

"Hell if I'm walking those," Lenny grumbled. But when she noticed she was the only one of their group who steered toward the escalator, she found the strength to veer back to the stairs.

"Look," Mr. Brown said to Greg. "It's the palace you've seen on the hill! Every night, my son's seen this lighted palace on the hill, and we've wondered what it was. And here it is! As if we've flown up through the night and into the day to find it."

"It's the Palau Nacional," Lenny said, without looking. "It houses a major art gallery." She brushed past them, grumbling to herself. *"Read a fucking book . . ."*

Olivia looked to her right as they strode up the promenade, an outsized landing between the first two flights of stairs. Looking up, she felt as if each flight was only a tiny inch forward. On the other side of a row of groomed trees, smaller fountains separate from the Magic Fountain spat at the sky, and the scent of fresh mist and mildew drifted coolly toward them. In the sun, the heat was just shy of wilting, and in the shade, the coolness was piercing, and in all places Miranda's presence seemed to squeeze her.

On the other side of the row of trees, children played behind a haze of flying water. Mothers called to them, but Olivia couldn't see the break in the barrier where they'd all gotten through.

"It's like in a museum," Marc said, nodding toward the row of trees. He slowed to join the Somersets, partly to keep them company and partly for a better view of the Browns catching up to Lenny. "The trees aren't a real barrier," he said, "but like the line on the floor in front of pictures in a museum, people think they can't pass through."

"It's such a nice pattern," Miranda said. "I like watching it go by."

Something in that set off Olivia, and she broke free from her sister's side. Miranda watched with mild panic as Olivia stepped quickly toward the others, then past them and ahead of them.

"Teenagers," Marc said, smiling.

The Palau Nacional sat atop the steep hill, large, domed, and dully orange. It grew out of the mist of the lone working fountain and rose in intricate layers with each flight of wide, shallow steps, which they climbed so achingly slowly they felt they were barely moving at all. The palace seemed to move like a king rising in a stately, grave manner to greet the peasants. But if they stopped to crane, pain would flood back into their thighs.

Olivia jogged forward with defiant freedom. A high, singing headache in her forehead gave an edge to the small scenes sliding past her. Up here, she could almost pretend she was alone and not followed by a damp, heavy load of companions and her sister. Each impact of her feet with the ground sent a bolt of pain into her head, but each soaring step gave her a brief sense of weightlessness that carried her through it.

She breathed the cool air deeply and shook back her hair. Mentally, she had already placed herself inside the Palau, safe and sheltered as a princess.

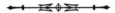

"Look, there's Olivia," Mr. Brown said to Greg. "She's gotten far ahead of us."

Greg merely shrugged and looked in another direction, not even noticing he was staring at a kid picking his nose.

"You could run up to her and talk. I don't mind," Mr. Brown said.

Greg turned back to his father with a faded smile.

"I'd rather stay here with you," he said.

"Hey Greg, is your dad okay with all these stairs?" Lenny asked. "You guys should go over to the escalator."

"I'm actually enjoying—"

"Come on, Dad," Greg said, slightly more perceptive than his father. "I'll go with you."

When they stepped onto the escalator together, Greg realized two things: how sore his own feet were, and what a relief it was to get away from Lenny, who didn't work very hard to hide her dislike. It almost made him want to laugh, even though it probably wasn't very nice. He chewed it over as he rose serenely through dust-shot light shafting toward the Palau. In the mottled sunshine, he put his hand on his father's shoulder and smiled faintly.

They were rising high above the bickering tourists. They were flying up through cloud and tree with an eerie cinema-crane quality, toward the dull gold Palau.

Olivia, in a final sprint, reached the terrace at the top before anyone else. As soon as she stopped climbing, her thighs boomed out in an ache that made her legs feel like lead, and her head spun with her empty stomach and the new sensation of standing still. She almost reached out for the balustrade, but only brushed her fingers on the cold stone. She straightened up as her heart sang to a staccato beat.

Below her, armies of steps crawled down and around the out-of-commission fountain. Above her, the Palau spread itself like a lion seated. And between them, the terrace rippled out, gray and cool. There was a coffee stand surrounded by low metal seats and lower tables, and there was a man playing guitar.

Chest heaving, eyes laughing, and free from the ground, Olivia turned and saw Greg and his father rising smoothly to her level. At first, they appeared like ghosts, vaporous and floating, and Olivia at that moment wouldn't question anything strange that happened, especially because she suspected that the man eerily tuning his guitar behind her was related to the accordion player near the Cathedral her first day. The guitar player's six tinny strings plunked and picked through the terrace like the whistling of an out-of-tune wind through tone-deaf trees—or possibly the voices of a chorus of ethereal birds with long, green wings. As her body coursed with energy, looking at the steps she had just climbed, Greg Brown came toward her, smiling because she was alone. Soon, he was standing near her, and now that she was free of Miranda, all of her guilt and anxiety melted with his smile.

She'd had no idea that her sister had that dampening effect on her.

The realization was only a short flicker in the spreading warmth through her limbs. As long as she was unwatched, she was free to feel what she wanted to feel. She briefly forgot that the others would eventually appear. She thought maybe, in the sound of the fountain, she could hear the sea again.

"I beat you up the stairs," she said, gasping.

"I took the escalator with my dad," he said.

"Oh, that's an escalator?" she said, peering around him. "It looked like you were stepping off the back of a bird."

"It *is* a bird. Can't you see it hovering? We just call it an escalator to avert a public panic," Greg said. "As soon as people know it's a bird, they'll all have an allergy."

Olivia laughed, and they looked down the hill together.

"Dad has trouble with steps sometimes," Greg said after a pause.

"You mean you got tired," said Olivia.

"I did not get tired. I'm not tired."

"You think you're a better climber than me."

"I never said you were a bad one," said Greg.

"I'll race you to the top of the palace steps."

His grin was the starting flag, and they sprinted off, dodging low-set metal chairs, svelte taut-faced women with paper cups of coffee, hordes of ecstatic children escaping the indoors, and a few disapproving attendants smoking cigarettes, until Greg touched the glass door of the art museum.

"I won!" he hollered.

"I got stuck behind a toddler with untied shoes," Olivia muttered.

"You should have moved him," Greg said, laughing.

They turned at the same time to look down at the terrace and steps. The man with the guitar continued to tune, but his tuning slid gradually into a canting, simple song that rose and fell rhythmically, vibrating gently across the terrace and up to the glass doors.

Looking farther down, Olivia saw Barcelona. She and Greg watched it together. But when Miranda, Lenny, and Marc crested the last steps with jolting strides, Olivia suddenly didn't want to be seen with Greg. Without speaking, she turned away abruptly and tried to lose herself in the loose crowd around the guitar player.

After a pause, Greg, a little dizzy with confusion, ambled across the terrace to find his father sitting in one of the low metal chairs, looking out of place.

"Did you have a nice race?" Mr. Brown asked pleasantly. Greg just sat beside him and interrogated the ground with his eyes.

As soon as the others broke away to visit the coffee stand, Miranda's gaze locked on her sister, and she made a beeline for her with the ruthless efficiency of an attack helicopter.

"Oh, there you are," she said. "Where did you go off to?"

"Here," Olivia said.

Lenny and Marc sailed over with drinks and snacks in hand.

"There's got to be some way we can lose the Browns," Lenny said.

"Can't you just drop it?" Olivia said.

As if on cue, Mr. Brown, across the terrace, noticed the group and hoisted himself out of his chair. Olivia had been watching the Browns out of the corner of her eye, but when Mr. Brown stood, she felt a jolt of guilt as if she had been caught staring, and she looked the other way.

In a matter of moments, he was there, dragging his son behind him. "Does anybody want to go in the museum?" he asked.

Marc's face brightened, and he was just about to respond when Lenny said, "I don't think the rest of us are into it, but if you want to, you should go. When else are you going to get a chance? You can catch up with us later."

Mr. Brown looked at Greg, and Greg, caught in a corner, was too startled to lie.

"I'd like to stay outside," Greg blurted.

"I think that's a great idea," Mr. Brown said, smiling at his son.

Lenny looked from one Brown to the other and back again.

"Well then," she practically growled, "let's go."

Lenny spun on her heels and struck out, leading the group away from the trembling glass doors, down the stately palace steps to the terrace at the top of the escalators, through the low metal chairs, out of the tremulous cloud of picked guitar strings, and toward the green on the other side of the Palau. They found a worn path that snaked around the right of the Palau, leading past a dusty little park to the Olympic complex and other attractions behind it. Marc clung to Miranda, and Miranda tried to cling to Olivia, but Olivia evaded her.

Looking straight ahead, Olivia didn't realize—until their paces had aligned—that Greg was also slightly apart from the clot of companions. He too had been looking directly ahead.

"My dad might get tired soon," he said, as if he felt he had to say something.

"Well, you should stop and buy him a cup of coffee," Olivia said, without slowing down to let him separate from her. "You can sit together and we'll come back down to you at the end."

"I don't want a cup of coffee," said Greg, who pulled even with her just as unstoppably. "And he's not allowed to drink it."

They walked in silence for a short stretch. Greg glanced at Olivia often. Olivia looked ahead.

"He's all right, as long as he has a place to sit when he needs a rest," said Greg. "And—and I like—I think he likes being around people. A big group of people. Nice people. Like you."

Olivia bit her lip. She didn't want to grin at the shy way he rambled. She wanted to feel annoyed so she could brush him off without feeling bad, like Lenny—only not really like Lenny. Maybe in a better, less mean way, because Lenny wasn't very nice and *Greg said I was nice people.*

The thing that made her afraid of Greg now was not Miranda's disapproval; Miranda was far behind. Something made her afraid of meeting his eye or touching his shoulder with her shoulder as they walked so close together that she felt the heat of his body next to hers. Maybe she'd like it too much and it would show.

She took a deep breath and said, "I don't know why I'm—we're so special." She stopped suddenly, realizing how egotistical that sounded. She started walking again, staring at the ground. "I mean, Miranda's made it so hard to be around me, and there are so many nicer people around."

When she didn't hear a response, she looked up and saw Greg looking at her in a way that answered why. She looked away again.

"Your sister talked to me last night," Greg said.

Olivia felt as though she had tripped over something large and hard. The others had long fallen behind, and Greg and Olivia were on a dusty yellow dirt path that led around the back of the Palau. The top of Montjuic was a wide, rippling plateau—even at the top, the path took them over rises and dips as they headed toward the other attractions on the crest.

Olivia tried to look more at the cacti and palm trees they walked between than at Greg as he spoke. Her lips trembled and her pulse hammered.

"She didn't seem—happy," he said. "And I thought maybe I could avoid you, if that's what you wanted. But then today, this morning, my dad didn't know. And by the time I found out we were all going together, it was too late, and then I saw you, and you looked different. Like you weren't happy, either."

"I had just woken up," Olivia said.

"Why are you so afraid of her?" asked Greg.

Olivia stopped dead in her tracks.

"Who?" she said.

"You know," he said.

"I'm not afraid of anyone," Olivia said, her voice growing shriller. "She's my sister. I trust her. And stop being nosy. This is our family. Go look after your dad."

Her heart hammered immediately, but she didn't take the words back. She wanted to feel powerful, like Miranda. She wanted to control the situation, like Miranda. She wanted for once to hold her ground, and holding it against Greg was less frightening than confronting Miranda—*no, not frightening*, she thought. *He can't be right.*

Greg looked away, kicked the dirt shallowly, and then looked up, stretching his neck. He folded his hands into his pockets and looked back down.

Then they both began to walk again. They couldn't help walking next to each other. Their paces broke and then aligned. A flight of pigeons rose up, flew across their way, and then swooped over and upwards to settle somewhere else.

She wondered if she resented him a little for going through worse times than her and coming out better.

"Do you feel different because you came here?" Greg asked. "You know, it just seems like things seem different once you've been somewhere out of your, uh, comfort zone."

"What the hell does that mean?" Olivia said, immediately regretting it.

Greg looked into her face, though she refused to tear her glance away from the path ahead of them.

"You sound like Lenny now," he said.

That landed like a slap in the face. At first, the only retort she could think of was a growl. Finally, she said, "I came here for a vacation, not a Lifetime movie."

They walked a little further—long enough for her to think of something else.

"I'm a boring person, okay?" Olivia said. "But I'm boring because I want to be. I like boring."

"You're not," Greg said simply. "You're not boring at all. You're not sleepy like they are—indifferent. Yesterday, when I saw you on the beach— when you were running to me—"

"I didn't run to you," Olivia said. "I was running to the water. I didn't see you."

"Okay. I didn't—I thought—I'm sorry," he said.

She felt a stab of guilt. He kept talking, for once unaware she was staring directly at him.

"I want to know who you are," Greg said, "because I think that person would be . . . someone kind of like me. Maybe not because you and me belong together forever or anything like that. But just because you have to try to experience something. I don't know. The point is that you did it, not that it was perfect, or right."

"I need to go," said Olivia. "Back to my sister. Leave me alone." She did not sound as confident as she'd hoped. Her heart was still pounding.

They rounded a corner and discovered the path had led them to the Olympic complex, a vast, desolate, and clean expanse of empty arenas, mammoth and cold.

Greg stopped abruptly, and so did she, as if she were tied to him with a string. The dirt ended at the edge of harsh gray cement, and Greg did not step over the line.

Behind him, the Palau hulked on its hill. Greg reached for her hand, but his fingers only brushed hers when the rush of her pulse told her to pull away and run toward the safety of the group.

Miranda and the rest had gained considerably, even with Mr. Brown in tow, and Olivia was out of breath when she stumbled to Miranda's side, back on the yellow dirt road. When she looked back, Greg was no longer where they had stood.

"Olivia! I was getting worried," Miranda said, though Olivia couldn't help suspecting that Miranda had only missed her as soon as she saw her. "Where were you?"

"So what is all this?" Olivia asked, flapping her hands at the monster arena dominating the swell behind the Palau. Her verve to change the subject made even Lenny look at her askance. Olivia hunched her shoulders as if to shrink from the attention she had just gained.

Taking a deep breath, she sat down on the edge of the curved ramp railing that snaked downward toward the rest of the complex. Tiny tourists just like her crawled over the concrete plains surrounding the buildings. The sun was so bright, she squinted until her eyes were nearly shut and her whole face pulled taut, her mouth puckering downward in an unconscious pout.

She took her pocket guide out of her shoulder bag, started flipping through it, turned it right-side up, and stared fiercely at the page on the Montjuic Olympic complex, snapping her head up and down to compare pictures with their subjects.

As Mr. Brown said something to the others, Olivia channeled all her attention into her book. Greg materialized from around a concrete curve, spoke with his father, and then struck off in the direction from which they had come. Mr. Brown lingered only a little longer, then set off after him, but not at a pace to suggest he meant to catch up. Miranda finally came toward Olivia's perch and filled her in.

"Lenny's relieved," Miranda said. "Looks like the Browns won't be coming with us after all."

"What? What did he say?" Olivia asked in one breath.

"Mr. Brown was getting tired already, and Greg seemed to think it was better for them if they made their way back and stayed close to the hostel."

"Oh."

Olivia looked out but was blinded by the light cast down by the sun and reflected up by expanses of glinting, simmering gray pavement. She imagined she saw two small figures on the dirt path, one taller, but it was probably just a residual image.

"So that's it," she said with a sigh.

"I hope you weren't too uncomfortable," Miranda said.

Olivia straightened with a pang. "*You* weren't," she snapped. "And that's all that matters."

"Olivia, I'm sorry if I—"

"You're always sorry," Olivia said, getting up. "I don't know why you keep saying that."

With a feeling like ice running down her back, Olivia wondered if she'd made the wrong decision in bowing to the group's judgment of the Browns. With the warmth of Greg's smile gone, the company of the others seemed bitter.

She marched up to Marc, cutting a clearly visible wake of frustration toward her sister. Marc only raised an eyebrow.

"Are we ready to go now?" Olivia asked.

"I think Lenny's flirting with those gentlemen, but I'd hate to interrupt her to find out," he said.

Lenny was chatting with two men in reflective gear leaning against a scaffold constructed around the entrance of the main arena. Olivia and Miranda watched her from a distance for a few minutes, waiting for her to return, before sending Marc out on reconnaissance. They watched from afar as Marc was promptly dismissed, and he returned almost immediately, looking slightly amused—as usual.

"No need to wait," he said. "Obviously, she's researching."

Miranda smiled tightly, and Olivia wasn't listening.

They set off again, along the sweltering concrete path away from the arena, gaining speed toward the nearest shade. The tabletop of the mountain rose now, revealing a little peak hidden by the Palau when viewed from the bottom. "How far is it up this mountain?" Marc asked with a laugh.

There weren't any signs that said "This far up the mountain," so the three travelers trekked slowly out of the Olympic complex, encountering a few double-backs and dead ends before they emerged fully and pointed themselves in the right direction.

The winding, deserted, quiet road ahead narrowed as it rose toward the botanical garden Miranda had read about in her guidebooks. At the garden gates, in the shade of a kiosk that looked vaguely like the visitor-information huts in national parks back in the United States, they bought their tickets in dense silence. The Jardí Botànic de Barcelona was a wide, rambling park of cacti, trellises, and Jurassic-looking spiny ferns draped over half a hillside, with a grade just steep enough to make walking up feel like work, even though it didn't look like it should be work. Once inside, Olivia made her way up a winding path and out of sight.

"We'd better look for her," Miranda said, and Marc, nodding, agreeably meandered away.

With his hands in his pockets, Marc looked down on telephone wires and chain-link fences and the roofs of the city, shy behind the hill at the edge of the garden enclosure.

Miranda, determined to see it all, walked through the *Californie*, *Chili*, and *Méditerranée occidentale* gardens, which is where she found a couple, horizontal on a bench tucked under the garden wall. Miranda was far more embarrassed than they seemed to be, if they noticed her at all.

Olivia was pacing in *Afrique du Sud*. Pink star-shaped flowers bobbed beside her, and she tried to concentrate on finding the right distance to stand from them so she could enjoy their scent without being overwhelmed by pollen and exacerbating her headache. She sat under the arbor of vines, got up and walked a few paces away, then came back and sat just outside the arch of flowers but found it was uncomfortable in the sun.

Getting up, she saw on the bricks of a pathway a trail of question marks, jauntily tilted, in all different sizes, leading down around a curve. She froze, but then the hammering of her heart sent her tiptoeing down the path, holding her breath.

Around the corner, behind a bush, a hunched figure worked with a piece of chalk, embellishing his question marks as they grew in size. The light shone in Olivia's eyes and for a moment she was stunned. What did it mean? She thought of the question mark she had found in her room at the hostel and felt a sudden irrational fear that the figure was Greg. Was it possible he hadn't gone back to the hostel? Why would he do this?

Suddenly, the boy stood and turned toward her. It was not Greg—it was some local boy, or a lone tourist, suddenly looking guilty. Behind him, Olivia saw that the question marks emanated from a phrase he had written, in Spanish, at the top of the walk. Olivia didn't know the words.

"What are you doing?" Olivia snapped at him, surprised at her own anger. "Why are you doing that?"

The kid bolted, dropping his chalk. Olivia stared after him, and then at the chalk. She touched it with her shoe, but didn't pick it up, and eventually she backed away. The rush of adrenaline fading, she wobbled back down the path from where she had come.

She thought of Mr. Brown's voice, full of enthusiasm in the morning, and how much he had looked forward to a nice day with people he'd thought had wanted him. She remembered the Cathedral, which felt like a month ago, and how eager Mr. Brown had been to keep her company and make her feel comfortable.

It was more than gratitude that generated her regret, though. Mr. Brown deserved to be treated kindly and gently because he couldn't understand why anyone would want to do otherwise, but it was only Greg who cared for him that thoroughly, consistently, and honestly.

Miranda thought the garden plants looked so desert-loving that they barely required enough care to be called "gardened." The dryness of their roots scrabbling into the dusty ground, the thick toughness of their husks, the spines and prickles, and the small, sterile-looking flowers made her homesick for the gardens she was familiar with—postage-stamp patches of irises, backyards lined with dogwoods and crape myrtles, azaleas and tulips, and the shady wooded bike trails by rivers lined with ferns. Miranda had hoped this would be a pretty garden, but it was just a nature garden.

As she prepared her complaints for Marc, she heard a sharp cry from the other side of the plot where she paced. Looking toward it, she saw Marc himself on his hands and knees, struggling up from the dirt—but he used only one hand, the other awkwardly crooked toward his chest. She hurried toward him.

"What happened?" she called when she was within a few yards.

Marc answered in strangled grunts as he flexed his arm and wrist, stopping the motion with a suppressed expletive.

"What's going on? Are you okay?" Miranda asked again.

"Tripped on something," Marc growled, blinking away the water that had welled in his eyes. "Caught myself funny on my hand. Think I busted up my wrist. Hurts like a . . . Hurts something awful."

Miranda looked down and around, discovering a big, round piece of sidewalk chalk, like the kind children play with, rolling down the gently graded path over a faded design on the bricks, indiscernible now.

"Is anything broken?" Miranda asked.

"I don't think so," he said. "Think I just jammed it. Might be a sprain."

Miranda fidgeted close to him, itching to do something.

"Let me see it," she said. "Maybe you can—maybe it's a—"

"I really think I should just get back to the hostel and wrap it up," Marc said. "An icepack and an ACE bandage should do it."

Marc started walking toward the garden's exit gate.

"Olivia!" Miranda said, first at Marc and then at the garden at large. "Olivia! We can't leave her behind!"

"You don't have to leave with me," Marc said, curtly through his pain. "I'm not an invalid. Stay here. I can go back alone."

Miranda ignored him, calling for Olivia until she finally emerged from a nearby trail, concern written across her face.

"What's going on?" Olivia asked.

"Marc hurt his wrist and we're going back to the hostel," Miranda said.

"You two should really stay and see the castle," Marc said through his teeth. "You came all the way up here and I'd hate for you to leave just because of me. It's not like you can do anything for me anyway."

Miranda blew off his objections with a shake of the head and continued following him. Olivia trailed behind.

A gardening truck rattled by, leaving behind its burned-rubber stink and an immovable grimy cloud. They moved out of its haze and through the exit.

The walk back down along the sides of the waterless Magic Fountain was a less vibrant rerun of the morning, and the pervasive noon sun made the stone-paved slope excruciating even for those travelers not suffering a sprain. There were two Metro lines to ride, both glinting and sharp-smelling.

It took an hour to get back. Olivia flung herself up the stairs, mumbling to her sister that she had a headache, and left her behind with Marc on the sidewalk, where they were scrutinizing various maps for hints about finding the nearest pharmacy. She had barely seen the Plaça Catalunya. She had barely seen the restaurant where her sister had treated her to dinner the night before. She had barely allowed herself to look at anything.

The squat, square door of Casa Joven was ajar, and she toppled into the lily-fragrant softness within. With the door, she nearly hit Sophie, who busied down the corridor with an armful of towels. Their eyes met.

Olivia felt as if she'd committed a crime.

Then she noticed the Browns sitting in the common room. Mr. Brown looked directly at her, a puzzled smile on his face.

"Is something wrong? You're back early," he said with genuine concern.

Greg merely started, stood briefly, looked as though he would escape, then sat back down again.

"Uh, no. Oh, well, Marc's hurt his wrist, but he's fine," Olivia whispered, fleeing to her room.

There, she was surrounded by the Browns again—the room they had given her and Miranda. The orange curtains diluted the harsh sunlight, and a rotating fan in the corner blew a breeze through the room, by turns fluttering her bed sheets and those of her sister. It reminded her of her room in childhood, in the long-ago days when summer was interminable and the humming bees and drifting pollen vibrated the sunlight until it was just right to sleep outside in the afternoon, though only under certain trees.

She slammed her fist on the bedpost when a sob escaped her. The day had gone terribly wrong, but so many of them had since the summers under the perfect trees.

Above all things, she missed her mom.

Miranda had seen her sister dart up the stairs to the hostel and, considering her safe, felt free to trail Marc to the closest pharmacy and back, dispensing small pieces of advice on sprains, medical attention abroad, and the various liability aspects of the garden's responsibility toward visitor safety.

At the door of the hostel, Marc told Miranda he was going to lie down until the pain meds he'd just bought kicked in, then left her there without waiting for a response. *That's what I get for trying to help*, Miranda thought.

Miranda hoped Olivia would be asleep by the time she got to the bedroom. Now, as she stood in the common room, she watched Mr. Brown reach out and pat Greg's knee, then return to his book. Greg had a book as well, but he was more captivated by some invisible point in the middle-distance outside the window. Something in the dark, empty look in Greg's brown eyes reminded her of her sister.

Miranda dropped her picnic-laden backpack on a kitchen table and raced for the bathroom.

She cleaned herself methodically. She picked the sand and dirt out from beneath her fingernails and toenails and scrubbed her face and the soles of her feet. She combed her hair into stick-like perfection and braided it tightly against the back of her head. She brushed her teeth, though she hadn't eaten anything since breakfast, and she cleaned her ears. She scrubbed herself back into feeling like herself, and it calmed her enough that she could approach Olivia.

It was barely half over, but the day was already as battered and bruised as the previous one had been.

Olivia wasn't sleeping. She was doing battle with her book. When Miranda slipped in, Olivia sat up immediately.

"How's Marc?" Olivia asked.

"Better. He'll be fine," Miranda said.

"Hey, do you think we can go up to the castle this afternoon? Just the two of us, so we don't have to deal with anyone else," Olivia said.

"I don't know. It would take all afternoon to climb up there again. Why didn't you say something earlier?"

"There's a gondola. I just found it on my transportation map. We must get there together. Come on, it'll be an adventure."

"I thought you had a headache."

"I'm better now," said Olivia. "I just remembered a part in one of my favorite books from middle school about a Spanish hill fort, and I thought maybe the castle is like that. It would be like visiting something from my book!"

"I think you should rest up, if you're not feeling well."

"I am feeling well!"

"We have all week," said Miranda. "We have plenty of time. We can take a break."

Olivia flopped backwards onto her bed again.

"I don't get it," she said. "You were so worked up about me seeing Greg again, and now you want me to stay in the hostel with him all day. It's like you want me to—"

"You haven't eaten anything today, have you? No wonder you have a headache. Come on, I'll fix you lunch."

Olivia scowled.

"It's important to show them you don't care they're here," Miranda said in her ear. "Otherwise, he'll think you're interested."

"I've tried that already, and he—"

"You can't spend the rest of our vacation hiding in our room, Olivia. You've got to eat, and I'm not bringing your lunch back here."

Olivia had little choice but to shuffle behind her sister into the common room, where Greg still lurked in the window corner under the sagging lilies. Mr. Brown was in the kitchen, attempting to have a conversation in broken Spanish with Hugo, who looked gently amused. Miranda sat her sister down at the table and began to unload the picnic things from her backpack.

"See, we have the place to ourselves," she said, not softly enough.

There were rolls and sliced ham and a block of cheese, battered water bottles and plastic forks. There was a bag of chips and a carton of juice, and Olivia let Miranda set everything out just as she had watched their mom set everything out for lunch on weekends in grade school. Everything they needed magically appeared from the cabinets, but it wasn't just a phenomenon of grade school. It was exactly what her mother had done for her just a few months ago.

Olivia picked at a squashed sandwich, the taste of warm plastic still clinging to it though the wrapper had been removed. She saw a steno pad on the corner of the table and idly flipped it open.

"Is that yours?" Miranda asked. "It doesn't look familiar."

"It's Lenny's," Olivia said. "I've seen her with it before. I wonder what she wrote about our trip."

Miranda wanted to know, too, but she was too mature to snoop for herself, so she let Olivia do it for her. Olivia craned her neck to see without touching the pages, but didn't read long. She scanned a few lines, and then her eyes flickered to Greg, who sensed the gaze and looked back with incomprehension.

Olivia pushed the notebook away and stormed to her room. Greg's eyes followed her, then looked questioningly at Miranda.

Miranda looked down at the page her sister had been reading and soon followed her out of the room. The remains of their forgotten lunch littered the table, wrappers and crumbs crowding around the notebook.

Mr. Brown and Hugo continued to murmur in the kitchen. Cars and tourists continued to wash down the streets outside. Laundry continued to float from backwards-facing balconies.

Greg sidled up to the table and looked at the open page.

He came from the sea and he kissed her, it read.

9

YOU'LL HAVE TO LOAN ME PAIN

"You told her all about it," Olivia said to Miranda, quietly but full of passion. "You were all about being good sisters and keeping things between ourselves and you blurted it all out to someone else. A journalist!"

"I was just—everyone needs someone to talk to—!" Overcome with embarrassment at being caught, Miranda didn't try to cover up. She had told Lenny on the walk up the mountain, when their mutual disdain for the Browns had reached its highest pitch.

"You have me! The whole point of this is you have me!"

"Olivia—"

"Don't say my name like that! Like I'm—like you're Mom. Like you still live at home and care about anything. You didn't even come home when Dad died."

"Was I supposed to wait at home until we heard from him? And you never even *knew* him!"

Olivia's eyes went wide. Miranda was shocked at her own forcefulness. Never had she actually criticized Olivia's feelings—only sought to protect them. But Miranda had carefully buried that week in her mind. She had so thoroughly rationalized her reasons for not attending the funeral that she assumed Olivia understood.

"We're both adults now," said Miranda. "Can't we get along?"

"We used to."

Miranda sighed and sat down on her bed.

"I'm going out," Olivia said.

"Where?"

"I don't know—I just need to walk. I don't want to be here anymore."

"Remember what I told you about wandering around alone."

"Well, if I don't remember, I'll just ask Lenny!" Olivia yelled.

"Do you want to talk about him?" Miranda asked with unexpected tenderness, just as Olivia's hand encircled the doorknob.

Olivia shot back a look that said *you're an idiot* more venomously and emphatically than any words could. Then she left.

It wasn't until Olivia was gone that Miranda realized Lenny hadn't yet returned, and therefore couldn't have written those words in that notebook. Someone else knew.

Greg had already vacated the common room, leaving his jacket draped across a chair. He took with him only his hostel keys, because they had never left his pocket, but as he left, he felt the only thing he really needed was not to be inside anymore.

Outside, he swam feverishly through crowds of blue-jerseyed football fans celebrating that night's game, flying blue flags and singing rude songs. He eased between pairs of mothers sorting out their children and restaurant reps hawking menus to passersby. He sliced through the fragrance first of fried calamari, and then of open flower stalls and the woodchips of gerbil cages. Through the worn soles of his shoes, his feet felt like stone. Water rushed above him and cast sprinkles on his face.

He was in the Plaça Catalunya. No question mark warned her that he might be there.

He said her name. She was there.

She was rooted to the spot and flowering, and he came toward her, sweeping through the seething crowd. He remembered her hand in his hand. He remembered the scent of lilies in his dream.

He captured her hand again. He shook the sea out of his hair. He held her against the tide of passing cars and football fans.

He kissed her in the Plaça Catalunya.

She pushed herself away from him and he realized he'd used up his last chance.

"Please don't do that again," she said. "Please stop bothering me."

"I didn't mean to—"

Olivia shoved him. She only meant to push him away.

But instead, he tripped backwards over his ankles, falling into the fountain behind him with a sickening crash. Olivia was afraid he'd cracked his head, but the clap was just the sound of water, his wide hands flinging out to catch himself.

Greg floundered, unable at first to get a footing or a handhold strong enough to rise from the slimy fountain.

A small crowd formed around them.

Greg rose at last, dripping and shaking, though the water wasn't very cold.

Olivia shook, too.

One of the onlookers gave a whoop of appreciation for Olivia. Another jeered.

The crowd around them tightened, but Greg's eyes fixed steadily on Olivia.

"I'm sorry," she said, but it only seemed to hurt him more. He, and the fountain, smelled strongly of chlorine.

He said nothing.

"I didn't mean to," Olivia said. But still Greg said nothing.

The crowd around them waited, but in a fury of shame, Olivia turned on her heels and ran away.

Olivia swept back to her sister, who was surprised and happy to see her back so quickly from her walk. And Olivia looked much more energetic, though in a slightly scary way.

"Let's go to Africa," Olivia said as she flounced onto the common room couch beside Miranda, plucking the book out of her hands.

"What?" Miranda asked.

"I want to go to Africa. I always kind of have. And it's so close from here," said Olivia. "We could cancel our last two days and go to Morocco or something."

"Morocco?"

"Yeah. Morocco, or Tunisia, or something. We don't even have to tell Mom we did it. We can come back for the last afternoon and fly back from here. It would be cool, like our secret adventure. You know, kinda like *Casablanca.*"

"Olivia, I don't think that's a . . . safe idea," Miranda said.

"American tourists go to Morocco all the time," Olivia said. "We don't even need a special visa or anything. We can get anywhere with our passports. And there are super-cheap flights from the airport here. I read about it in one of the guidebooks."

"I really think we should call Mom first," Miranda said. Her heart hammered, worrying that she'd set off another episode. But nothing Olivia had said so far was irrational—just impulsive. In fact, she seemed to have thought through some very real details.

"Don't call Mom," said Olivia. "She'll say no, and then we'll never have the chance to go to Africa again. Together!"

Olivia put her arms around Miranda, rested her cheek on her sister's shoulder, and gave her a tight squeeze.

"Please," she said, more urgently. "I've always wanted to do this, Miranda. You can't stop me."

"What about all the friends we've made here?" Miranda said. "Aren't you having fun with them?"

Olivia pulled away and crossed her arms.

"Seriously?" she said.

Miranda leaned back as if slapped, and looked at her sister for a long while. "I'll talk to Hugo this afternoon about checking out early," Miranda finally said.

She got up, but on impulse, she whirled around and knelt in front of Olivia, holding her face in her hands. Olivia bit her lips into her mouth.

"Try to take a nap," Miranda said. "You look warm, and you don't want to come down with something while you're away from home."

"I think I've slept more here than I ever do at home," Olivia said.

"Jet lag," Miranda said, getting up again and giving her sister a proprietary pat on the head.

As Miranda went to look for Hugo, Olivia cast a mental spell to make him indiscoverable. She drank in her solitude, laid her feelings on the couch beside her, and looked at them carefully. The closest she had come to this kind of confusion was the numbness that had deadened her that day, about nine months ago, when she'd stared at the acceptance letter from Cornell University. Four years of furious work, careful planning, deadlines, essays, nights of studying, and rigid scheduling, and now she'd held the results in her hands and realized, for the first time, that she didn't know what she wanted to do with her life.

She only knew she didn't want to leave home.

After a few trips up and down the main hall, Miranda found Sophie in the kitchen, draining the water from the lily vase.

"Where's Hugo?" she asked as if it were Sophie's fault he couldn't be found.

Sophie shrugged and frowned, pushing the pedal for the faucet to flow, refilling her vase with fresh water.

"Do you know where the Browns are?" Miranda asked impulsively.

This time the answer was an impatient sigh as Sophie glided back into the common room, carrying her flowers to their place in the back. Olivia had disappeared. Sophie opened a window, sat at the computer, and sternly ignored Miranda until Miranda decided to ignore her.

Miranda sat herself on the couch where Olivia had been and waited for anyone at all to arrive.

It was Lenny who next swung open the door with self-satisfied gusto, meeting Miranda's glare.

"What, did someone die?" she asked, her hangover apparently having abated at last with the help of two stunning young men in reflective gear.

"No, I'm just waiting for everyone to get back," Miranda said.

"Lonely are we?" Lenny said, dropping her bag onto a chair and rounding the corner to her dorm. Her voice emerged: "You're trying to catch someone."

Soon, she followed her voice back into the common room.

"Have you seen Hugo around?" Lenny asked. "I need to talk to him."

"No. I'm waiting for him, too."

"What's up?" Lenny asked, plopping down beside Miranda. Miranda got up and began to clear away the debris of her picnic lunch.

"Olivia saw someone's notebook. Someone's been writing about her," said Miranda, picking up the notebook to show it to Lenny. "Her and *Greg*."

"Her and Greg?" Lenny asked.

"On the beach. You know," Miranda said, anger flaring higher at Lenny's nonchalant non-reaction.

"Weird," Lenny said with raised eyebrows.

"No, you don't get it!" Miranda said, slapping the notebook back to the table. "I know you told someone. Who else here knows?"

"Hey, hold up, calm down," said Lenny. "I haven't told anyone."

"That's impossible. It's right here!"

"I don't know who wrote that," Lenny said, "but it wasn't me, and I didn't tell them."

Miranda felt a rush of relief. "I'm so glad it's not my fault." She sighed. "Or yours, either," she added. "Olivia thought it was you. I knew I could trust you."

"Well, don't get too attached," Lenny said with a grin. "I'm going to Tarragona tonight. That's why I'm looking for Hugo. I need to check out. I think I might just leave a note."

"I thought you were staying until the end of the week," said Miranda. "You have an article to write."

"On Catalonia. Not just Barcelona," said Lenny. "I thought I might as well start on day trips. One of the guys I met today has family up there and he said he'd show me around."

"He could be anyone!" Miranda said. "Are you going to stay with him?"

"It's my job," Lenny replied, hopping up. "I'll be okay. I've got to go pack up. The train leaves at 4:30, and I'm meeting Sam at the station." She ran out, then quickly returned to the common room with a brimming backpack and a half-rolled sleeping bag. She threw her things onto the floor and began unpacking and re-sorting her underwear by Miranda's feet.

"Marc's in there and he's snoring," Lenny said. "You guys must have climbed that mountain pretty fast!"

"We did, I guess, but we skipped the castle."

Lenny just snorted and shrugged, and left her boxer-pajamas hanging out of her bag's outer compartment while she ran into the kitchen and snatched a bottle of water from the fridge.

"Hey, do you mind leaving a couple euro for Hugo for this?" she said. "I'm completely out of change."

"Have you ever been to Africa?" Miranda asked.

"Lived in South Africa a little while. Why?"

"How about Morocco?"

"Too many Americans," Lenny said. "You'd probably like it. It's a nice . . . safe place to go if you really want to visit Africa."

"Do you know if there's a good hostel there we could stay at?"

"I think I know someone," said Lenny. "I don't think he runs a place, but he knows whoever does, or something like that, and I've heard about it. Sounds nice. Your kind of nice."

"Do you have his number?"

Once she convinced herself this needed to be done and calmed down enough to do it, Miranda realized there were only really three things to worry about. First: Find a place to stay. Next: Find a way to get there. Last: Get away from *here*. It was almost too easy.

Lenny stared at her. She had just said something.

"What?" Miranda said.

"I didn't know you were into Africa," Lenny repeated.

"Oh, yeah. Olivia's always wanted to go."

"Huh. I guess I thought she would have mentioned it sometime. Since it's so close to here, you know."

"Yeah. We can't wait."

Lenny laughed. "I can't believe Olivia never asked me about Africa. You'd think she would, right?"

"Sure."

"I mean, if you'd mentioned it earlier, I probably could have helped you out a lot more. But now I've got plans . . ."

"It's okay."

Lenny concentrated for a moment on untangling three socks from a bra.

"I know she'll love it," Lenny said with a smirk. "If you don't come back changed after that place . . ." She shrugged, as if that was all that had to be said.

Lenny left that afternoon without saying goodbye, without leaving a note for Hugo, and, it was found out later, without paying half her bill. The only address she left was the editorial office of *Lonely Planisphere*. The magazine, it turned out, had been defunct for eighteen months.

"Lenny left this for a bottle of water," Miranda said when she finally found Hugo a bit later, leaning over Sophie at the computer as she worked out how much the hostel had lost from the backup funds they kept for walk-outs. Miranda put down two euro of her own money.

Sophie's eyes narrowed slightly, but Hugo still had his arm around her, and his thumb found its way up and then down again, fanning against her side. She bit her lip while he smiled away Miranda. So few people actually paid for the water they took that they'd stopped charging, Hugo explained. Miranda could take the euro back.

Miranda stood, staring at the coins, wondering whether it would be worse to leave them or worse to take them, but eventually she slid them back off the desk and into her pocket. She turned and slunked away, but came back immediately when she remembered what she had actually wanted Hugo for.

"What's your policy on terminating a stay early?" Miranda asked.

"What?" Sophie said.

"If I want to leave. Can I have my money back?"

Sophie shot daggers at her.

"No, sorry," she said. "No cancellation after the booking is confirmed."

Miranda sighed.

"Can't you just give our room to someone else?"

"No cancellation."

"But you *are* just going to give our room to someone else!"

Hugo shrugged and shot a glance up at Sophie. Rolling her eyes, Miranda stalked to the computers at the back of the common room, where she looked up Lenny's friend's friend's friend's hostel in Casablanca, Morocco, and then took notes on budget flight schedules.

"I've booked us a room in Casablanca, and a flight on Econair for tomorrow morning," Miranda said to the back of Olivia's book as she strode into their room. The book bobbed, which Miranda saw as a positive response until she realized Olivia was just turning a page.

"Great," Olivia eventually said.

"Come on, don't you want to go out and buy a guidebook to celebrate?"

"They'd all be in Spanish."

"What the hell, maybe my leftover college Spanish isn't as useless as I thought. It'll be an adventure." But Miranda felt the same rising fear she'd experienced when she'd first seen her little sister unresponsive in bed. At each step of Olivia's improvement, there had been a little backslide before the plateau.

"I'm tired. I think I'll read here," said Olivia.

"Well, we need something to tell us where to go," Miranda said. "But if you don't feel well, you rest here. I'll be back in a few."

Miranda revolved out of the room. Her actions were mirrored by sleep-tousled Marc across the corridor. He grinned at her, noting the coincidence with a nod, which encouraged her to smile as well. Maybe it was waking up and looking so disheveled, but he seemed more welcoming and less flippant than he ever had before, even before opening his mouth. His wrist was wrapped neatly in an ACE bandage, and the pinched look was gone from his eyes.

"How are you doing?" Miranda said, a protective edge still lingering in her tone.

"Oh, this? Much better," Marc replied, brandishing his bandaged arm. "I'm not sure what worked best—the bandage, the ice, the nap, or the meds—but I feel much better—about the world at large, as a matter of fact," he said, slightly dreamily.

"You know, they sell much stronger stuff over-the-counter here than they do back in the States," Miranda said suspiciously. "Well, I guess you know that, since it's sort of the same in Peru, right?" She'd forgotten for a second that he wasn't American like her.

Marc blinked.

"Oh, yes, of course," he said after short consideration. "Where are you off to?"

"I'm looking for a bookstore," she said. "Olivia doesn't want to go out again."

"A bookstore? I'll come with you. I love bookstores. Just give me a minute."

"Really, don't you want to sleep it off a little—"

"I'll only be a second," said Marc. "Let me put on a clean shirt."

Miranda retreated to the common room and stood between the kitchen tables, shifting from foot to foot. She tried to avoid looking in either direction, because Hugo anchored one end of the front hall, shuffling calculations on the reception laptop, and at the back of the room, Sophie simmered at one of the guest computer stations.

The lilies were gone. Either they had expired quickly or Sophie had taken them home. All that remained was a damp brown circle on the sill where they used to sit. If it were spring, Sophie could have opened the window and put out a box where she could grow fresh flowers and watch them bloom through the grainy-streaked glass, yawning above stories of green leaves. Miranda grew red geraniums in her balcony garden at home, and she liked looking into her neighbors' window gardens.

Five minutes later, Marc appeared in a black t-shirt and black jeans, looking slightly more combed. With the late-afternoon sunshine illuminating his gray-threaded black hair, he looked charming, and reminded her of what people seemed to see in Hugo. She remembered with a jolt that he had said he was becoming a priest. Every day, every hour, each new appearance he put in, he seemed more relaxed, more average, and less like a priest, as if his character were softening in the sun and sloughing off in waxy peels.

Did travel do that to people? Was it doing it to Olivia?

"We are ready to embark," he said, beaming a manic grin at Miranda and swinging his arms, stopping himself with huge eyes just before clapping his hands together.

Miranda smiled tightly and looked to the door. They left.

In the cool noisiness of the shady street, Miranda felt the pressure in her chest lift. She looked around herself without a camera in hand and enjoyed what she saw. Now that she knew she'd be leaving shortly, she could finally enjoy being there. She let the late afternoon trickle of the crowd wash her gently down the street, and barely cared whether Marc kept up, except to see his grin and nod every so often when they passed something they both liked or found funny.

Miranda turned into a travel bookshop hidden in a nook between two larger buildings, but Marc stopped her at the door.

"Everything in here's going to be in Spanish," Marc said. "If you're looking for something to read, I think there's a bookstand with English paperbacks just around the corner."

"I have something specific in mind," Miranda said, sweeping to the back corner of the shop.

Marc followed with considerable curiosity. "The bookstand has some guides," he said.

"Just Barcelona and Spain stuff," Miranda said, entering the Africa section.

"Planning another trip already? Can't you buy a guide when you get home?"

"We're not going home," said Miranda. "Well, we're going home, but we're leaving first. To Casablanca."

"You got a few extra days off?"

"No, we're leaving here early. Our flight is tomorrow morning."

Marc's face extended downward in a thoughtful frown, and he leaned against the bookshelf behind him. He stood and stared at her for several moments without making a comment.

Confused, Miranda turned back to her shelf and read through each title meticulously, even when she didn't know what they meant. She had the crawly, damp sensation down the back of her scalp of covering something up.

"Is there something wrong?" said Marc. "I thought you were enjoying it here. Why the sudden urge to get away?"

"We're not getting away from anything," Miranda said quickly. "Olivia and I have always wanted to go to Africa."

"Ah, it must have been Olivia's plan. This doesn't sound like you. Or maybe I read you wrong," Marc said.

"What does that mean?" Miranda avoided Marc's eyes by staring intently at a book she had just pulled down. Realizing she held it upside-down, she gave up and put it back on the shelf without ever determining what it was about.

Marc pushed himself upright again and shrugged.

"It doesn't matter. I was just curious," he said. "It just sounds like something—something Lenny would do. Did she talk you into it?"

"Lenny left a few hours ago," Miranda said.

"Well that explains the silence." Marc laughed weakly. "You two looked like you got along pretty well. Aren't you upset she's gone early?"

"We're going, too, so it doesn't really matter," said Miranda. "Anyway, the week's half over, and Olivia really wants to get out and see something different while she has the time. To tell the truth, so do I." Miranda approached the counter with a pocket-sized map and guide to Casablanca written in fourth-grade-level Spanish.

"That sounds like a lot of fun," Marc said blandly. "I can't blame her, on her first trip out of the country. Isn't that what she told me?"

"Yeah, that's right."

Miranda counted her change and paid in part with the money she'd taken back for Lenny's water. She sailed out of the store and into Marc's puzzled smile.

"How are you going to read that?" Marc asked, referring to the book she'd just bought.

"I knew a little Spanish back in college," Miranda said. "It's easier to remember how to read it than how to speak it. It's enough to get directions at least."

"Too bad. You could have practiced your speaking here," Marc said, turning sharply to begin their march back to the hostel.

They walked slowly, and Miranda felt the shadows drop over her and onto the pavement. She remembered the last time she had felt her surroundings to be so magical. It was when she was twelve, drawing with colored chalk on the sidewalk in front of her house—giant crabs and seascapes and smiling faces. The rumble of the thick chalk over pebbly concrete was like the earth quaking, and the flight of birds from the tree above was the flight of her hair in the summer breeze. Miranda brushed it aside with a wisp that escaped from behind her ear.

She thought of her sister as she had found her yesterday morning, curled around her book in a chair, asleep.

Olivia was changing. She felt it sometimes when she woke up and creaked her joints, and looked down the length of her body to the tips of her toes, and wondered, *When did this happen to me?* She thought it sometimes when she put down her book and looked around her and saw that everything was completely different.

The solid black letters slid out from under her eyes and once more uncovered the room. Olivia's head hurt now, and she wanted a glass of water. She sat up slowly, hyperaware of the bed's squealing springs, the moan of the floorboards under her feet, and the crinkle of fabric across her skin. Her mouth tasted sour, and she remembered she had hardly eaten any lunch, but the sun had dried all the hunger out of her. Now she only wanted to lie somewhere very dark and pass out, only she needed water first.

Hugo was waiting. Olivia blinked. She was suddenly aware of the possibility of pillow marks on her cheek. Her mouth opened and it closed, while Hugo waited, looking inquisitively into her puzzled eyes.

"Drinking water?" she asked at last.

He nodded and opened the fridge where the water bottles were, and then got a glass down for her and poured some out. He handed it to her and watched her drink, and she gave him the glass when she was done, her head spinning.

"Thank you," she said.

"No problem. Have a nice trip tomorrow."

The words hit Olivia in the chest with a dull thud. She swallowed it. Her heart began to pound. It was unpleasantly hot and sticky, standing in the kitchen facing Hugo.

"Thanks," she said again. Hugo held her with his open, friendly gaze, impossible to escape.

"You must really want to get out and see more," he said. "I hope you have a good time."

Olivia felt her face working.

"I just feel like we're done here," she said, shrugging. "We've seen everything."

"You can't. Have you gone up to the castle?"

"Yes. It was very nice, and we're done now," Olivia lied.

Hugo frowned slightly and drew down his eyes.

Olivia's throat was tight and her dizziness increased.

"I have to go pack," she said breathlessly, whirling away.

In her room, Olivia stopped to stare at her suitcase in the corner, clean and dirty clothes spilling out. Crumpled pamphlets were strewn across the floor, and her shoes were upside-down under the bed. She shut the door and was terrified.

She hadn't seen Barcelona, and now she was leaving it—the place that had made her so thoroughly homesick and confused, the place that had shocked her with new, beautiful, and hopeful things. It reminded her of the last day of fifth grade, and feeling the dull, thick sense of indefinable grief that another year was slipping by, moving steadily through childhood and toward something gaping, black, and unknown. Even then, Olivia had always been sadder at the end of the school year than at the end of summer.

She thought about the roof of the cathedral. She remembered the way she'd treated Mr. Brown. Then she thought of how Hugo already knew their travel plans, and how they also had to say goodbye to everyone else they knew at the hostel, and realized that Miranda had probably done all of the lying for her before she even knew they were lies.

Olivia fell to her knees, hard, and dragged the suitcase out. She barely knew where to begin, so she unpacked everything slowly, and laid it out on her bed as she had the night before she'd left home. She made a pile for shirts and a pile for jeans, and a heap of socks and a mound of underwear. Then she swept all the dirty items into a plastic bag that she buried at the very bottom of her suitcase. With that hidden away, everything else looked neat, and the order calmed her and numbed her singing nerves.

Each rigid movement, swiveling between the bed and the open suitcase, followed a steady tempo. The words *you're leaving in the morning* marched with a Metronome beat. Her heart slowed to the rhythm of her packing, and when the bed was clear, she fell into it. When at last she blinked her sore eyes, she felt a tear oozing out of the corner of one of them.

There was a light knock, and then the door creaked. With a surge of adrenaline, Olivia threw herself onto her other side, facing the wall. She didn't want to speak to Miranda, but she couldn't bring herself to feign sleep, so she stared dry-eyed at the bumpy whiteness of the wall in front of her nose and waited for her sister to leave again.

But it wasn't Miranda, she realized as the thinness of the shadow passed across the wall. It was Sophie, dropping off a stapled receipt. When the door shut again, Olivia was alone, and she set her hand against the wall, turned her face into the pillow, and lay still and tense.

Their last night in Barcelona closed as drearily as a chill, drizzly November day in the dripping hills of Virginia. The sun, veiled by the haze of pollution and discontent, set, restless and unwatched.

10

A FRAGILE CERTAIN SONG

There were suitcases in the hall. They did not belong to the Somersets, because Miranda insisted on keeping their bags in their room, with her, until they were ready to check out, to protect them against the negligible possibility of theft.

The bags in the hall belonged to Ana and Chas, the Polish couple—they were also leaving that day, to continue the tour they'd planned, and Miranda was silently thankful, because it made it easier for her and her sister to slip out unnoticed.

She felt a jolt of jealousy, however, noticing how much other people seemed to *care* that Ana and Chas were leaving—how they all took the opportunity to exchange e-mail addresses and plan to meet again somewhere else. But Miranda had long ago concluded she just wasn't popular or easily likeable, so, if she were to leave unnoticed, it would be by her own choice, and she would be unmissed.

Ana and Chas's departure also drew the Browns out of the dorm room. Mr. Brown held Ana's hand and spoke quietly to them both, a crinkly smile on his face, while his son hung back and blinked nervously. When at last the couple picked up their bags—the Browns were the last to wish them well—Greg clapped Chas on the shoulder and nodded. He hadn't spoken a word the whole time.

Olivia, who observed it all from the dining table, was thankful for that, because, in her own unconscious and breathless way, she feared hearing his voice. She studied her cereal closely, as it went soggy around the edges, bubbles of milk floating lazily up when she lifted and then dropped her spoon. She felt him there all the while, in the same way she had sensed him whenever he had been near—a warmth that began just below her breastbone and exploded down to the tips of her fingers.

She had been sensitive to his comings and goings, even when doors were between them. She had lain in her bed all the night before, wondering when he would creep down their hall, and if he had ever come back from the Plaça Catalunya, though she understood that even Greg Brown wasn't so abnormal that he would run away while on vacation. Would it all hurt less, she wondered, if she just stayed, *with* him?

But there he was, and he wasn't looking at her, either. Olivia was engulfed by last night's dreams—by the vague hope that, despite all the confusion, he would appear; that something would happen, something large, and that would tell her whether to stand up and smile at him or just to go.

They had an hour before they had to leave for the airport. Olivia had woken early because she couldn't sleep, but having packed the night before, she had nothing to do to kill time while waiting out here for Miranda.

There was nothing to distract her from the gnawing fear that Greg would drift toward her and start talking, or maybe ask her why she was going. When Greg followed his dad back to the dorm room, Olivia set down her breakfast and darted for her own room.

"Do you want to take a walk?" she asked Miranda, stepping into the room.

"I still have a few things to do," Miranda said into her coffee mug.

Olivia felt the same stifling rage as yesterday.

"What can you possibly have to do?" she said. "I want to look around one last time."

"I have to finish packing and settle up with Hugo."

"Well, you can do that while I go take a walk."

"Olivia, I'd really rather you wait here. You don't want us to be late and miss our flight," Miranda said.

Olivia pouted, and as she began to return to the common room to clean her dishes, she turned around and grabbed Miranda's coffee mug from out of her hands.

"I'll clean this for you," Olivia said over her shoulder. She was in the kitchen rinsing it out before Miranda could even open her mouth, and soon, Olivia was furiously washing everything in the sink.

She had started with her own dishes, but as she set them in the drying rack, she was seized by a familiar fear. It was the fear of a girl in her bed the morning she was supposed to leave her childhood home and learn to be a grown-up.

As long as there was something else to clean here, something else to set right, as long as she stayed here at this sink with the water running over her hands, she wouldn't have to take another step toward an ending.

Her lungs caught the feeling and wanted nothing to do with air. Her breath slowed until the air merely pulsed up and down like ripples in a bathtub.

The kitchen went softly out of focus, her eyes fixing on the sign above the sink, until it seemed to float off the wall, or perhaps the wall drifted away from behind it.

The sign said, "Have you Cleaned what you Used??"

The sink was empty. Olivia's foot rested heavily on the pedal that made the water run.

Punctuation—a sign without a sound.

A small voice inside her said, "Not now," but she didn't listen. She was already on the slide.

The sound of water had covered over the sound of Miranda closing their door. It had covered over the shuffle of Hugo's disappearing into the private end of the hostel. Now it covered over the creak of floorboards as Greg Brown entered the common room, but it couldn't cover over the shiver that darted down Olivia's arms as he appeared behind her, like the first jolt of consciousness when waking in the morning.

She lifted her foot and the water stopped, but her hands were still dripping.

As if an invisible hand held her chin, she looked up. Her eyes met his eyes. They stood, looking and seeing each other, dripping, frozen in the crisp morning light.

Then she breathed deeply. He stepped toward her.

Miranda, in her room, was not packing. She was looking at the piles of her things stacked neatly on the bed: the old clothes she'd brought with her and the new gifts she had bought yesterday night—a fan for her mother and candies for her coworkers. She looked at the carefully alphabetized and flattened pile of pamphlets, tourist information, and ticket stubs, and at the Spanish-language Casablanca guidebook sitting next to it. She looked at her shoes, upright and straight on the floor at the foot of her bed. She looked at her jacket, neatly aligned next to her open suitcase. With all these things together and in order, the room seemed barren, wounded. She'd thought the room would seem bigger, but it actually felt smaller.

The window emitted only a square foot of petrified light. The orange curtains were faded and dusty. The floorboards between their beds were worn and splintered near the door, and standing in the middle, she could touch each bed with her hands, bending over pertly like a ballerina at the barre.

She began to place her possessions quickly but neatly into her bag. They fit perfectly.

The door hung open a crack, and it creaked open another inch when someone outside tapped on it gently. Miranda assumed it was Olivia and wondered why she would bother knocking. She called out for her to come in.

Mr. Brown poked his head around the door, and the rest of him followed sheepishly. It seemed foolish in a man his age, but Miranda had little room left to be petty.

"I think Greg left something in here," he said as he came in. "But he won't come and get it, and I don't understand why, if it was that important, he didn't notice it missing before. Have you found anything since you've been here?"

"I wouldn't know what to look for," Miranda replied in a daze.

"I think it was a piece of paper. We always have plenty of paper—we bring notebooks everywhere—but this one seemed important."

"Notebooks," Miranda said, and the word triggered the memory of yesterday's discovery in the common room. Her blood ran hot. "It was your notebook! You—you—I can't believe you'd write that about my sister—about your own son!"

Mr. Brown sat down and looked at her with a contracted brow. The folds of his face molded around incomprehension and concern.

"Wrote what?" he said. "Slow down and explain it to me."

"The notebook on the kitchen table. My sister saw it yesterday. I told her not to, but what she read in it was about her." Miranda took a deep breath. "It was about Greg kissing her. The other day. On the beach."

Mr. Brown's face lit up, which was not the reaction Miranda had been hoping for. "Greg and your sister?" For a moment, he was unable to express himself. Then, he began to laugh. "Well, that's kind of sweet, isn't it? Isn't it nice they found each other?"

"No!" Miranda exclaimed.

"But don't you think leaving early is breaking her heart? Hugo told me about it last night," said Mr. Brown. "And I can see it's breaking *your* heart." He leaned forward.

Miranda recoiled.

"I'm sorry, I don't think you understand at all," she said, crossing her arms.

"Why are you running away?" Mr. Brown pressed, implacable. "Is it someone you've met? Is it Marc?"

Miranda was furious with a passion she hadn't felt in years. Her eyes flamed, and fire bubbled up her throat.

"It isn't always about a boy!" she snapped, a tenseness in her shoulders and her jaw. She held herself rigidly. "Sometimes you don't want it to be about a boy."

"What happened?" Mr. Brown asked with irritating gentleness.

Miranda stomped. She bit her lips, looked at the ceiling, and shifted from foot to foot.

"Why should I have to tell you anything?" she finally asked.

"You don't."

Miranda glanced out the window. She'd never really looked at the view before. The window was just above the adjacent roof, and she saw birds settling on the chimney of the building next-door, dirty and disheveled. The sunlight was not direct, but through the translucent curtains, she felt its diffused glow illuminate her face forgivingly.

"Travel romances never work. I know. I met a boy in Madrid. He told me he wanted to come and stay with me back home. I went home and never heard from him again." It gushed out unbidden. She'd never even told Olivia.

"It isn't about the boy," Mr. Brown echoed, standing and offering his seat on Olivia's clear bed to Miranda. She scowled at him but couldn't refuse. She felt twelve years old, being ushered from place to place.

"Let me guess—you never wrote to him, either." Mr. Brown knelt in front of her, taking her hands.

"*He* promised *me*," she said. "I never promised anything."

It was there again, everything she had felt, the static prickle when he—the boy from Madrid—had entered a room, wanting him so much it had scared her. So she had left him, let it drop, and sunk back into the comfortable numbness of everyday life. She'd made the cut cleanly, and bled until she was dry and impervious, and everything turned normal again.

But the blood bubbled up again, and boiled behind her eyes and made her burn. She snatched her hands away but instantly regretted it. She looked into Mr. Brown's eyes.

"Why did you come back to Spain?" Mr. Brown said gently.

"I really liked Spain," Miranda said. "I think I wanted to prove it wasn't just because of him. But we're going to Africa now . . ."

"You don't have to," he said. "Your room is still yours. You have a place to stay."

"But Olivia wants to go to Africa," Miranda said. "She was so desperate to get away, and I did it to her."

"You were only trying to be a good sister," Mr. Brown said. "She'll understand. You could have done worse."

"I don't think she'll understand," Miranda said, sniffling. As an afterthought, she added, "I don't think she ever really understands. Something always gets lost between us."

Olivia's breakdown that summer had dredged it all up. She could have tried harder to find a job in Williamsburg. She could have tried to move Olivia to live with her in Arlington. She could have come home for the funeral. She could have been a better sister. But all along she had wanted only to make herself feel better.

Mr. Brown heaved himself up to his feet, and Miranda jumped to help him. He dusted his knees.

"You don't always have to know everything about each other's hearts and minds," he said as her hand remained on his shoulder. "But at least you can accept it."

"Accept what?"

He just smiled.

As they stood together, Miranda gradually recovered her stability and began to feel her age. She could shrug off Mr. Brown's last piece of rambling wisdom as she used to shake off his kindness, but this time it was with patience rather than flinty disrespect. She didn't think Mr. Brown would mind.

In the settling silence, she remembered why Mr. Brown had come in. "Weren't you looking for something?" she asked him.

Mr. Brown paused, looking slightly puzzled.

"Oh, well," he said, with a twinkle that made Miranda wonder if it was all a ploy. "It doesn't matter now that you're staying."

Then he shuffled out of the room as quietly as he had come.

With a sigh, Miranda settled back into the bright and happy morning.

A sigh rippled like a breeze through the corridors and corners of the hostel and filtered through the empty common room, settling on the place where Greg had stepped forward and caught Olivia's dripping hand. She looked up at him, so close now.

"You caught me," she said quietly. "You win."

"Were we playing something?"

"You weren't," Olivia said, a smile dawning on her face.

He smiled at her smile and leaned his cheek on her hair.

"Can I talk to you now?" he asked, gently tugging her toward the empty dormitory. "Can I get to know you?"

"Yes," Olivia said.

In the place where they had been, their warmth lingered.

When Miranda strolled into the common room, the place was empty, drops of water still fresh on the kitchen floor. The window at the back rattled, and Miranda opened it herself, because it looked like it was going to be a warm day. The curtains flapped against her face. Just for one second, the world was orange.

She realized she didn't know where her sister was.

Miranda ran into the dormitory to ask Marc or Mr. Brown, but she stopped in the door.

Against the light of the back window, silhouetted against the orange curtains, she saw Olivia's ear against his heart. She saw his cheek on her hair. She heard the soft murmur of their voices. She gathered all she needed to know about Olivia wanting to go to Africa.

She stepped quietly out again.

Mr. Brown was not to be found in the common room or the kitchen. He had probably gone in search of someone else's life to change. Alone, she lay down on the couch and spotted Olivia's novel on the end table, forgotten. She picked it up and flipped to the bookmarked page.

She remembered reading this book in eighth grade, and having it read to her by her father years before. She remembered how tense she'd felt during the scary parts, though she no longer could remember what happened. She remembered believing that real life was like that, and asking whether she would find the same concepts in the encyclopedia. Later, when she was a bit more grown-up, she would wince with embarrassment at the desperation of her imagination, and her gullibility—but after that, she would laugh and tell the story to her friends, a decibel too loudly, when they talked about how stupid they had been when they were little. Now, she could look back on these things as if that girl were a different person—blameless, sheltered, and honest—who believed in novels and sought adventure tales, if not adventure itself.

The sun defined itself high in the sky, and as it flew, it gained in color and intensity.

Finally, the wide, squat door of the hostel was nudged open, and the world breezed in, in the form of Marc, who bore a paper coffee cup and a brown bag stained with oil and sugar.

He stopped with a faltered step, and it was quiet enough for Miranda to hear his coffee slosh forward as if eager to be other places.

"I thought you were your sister for a second," he said, and then, after another tense pause, "Aren't you supposed to be in Africa?"

Miranda let the book drop onto her chest and looked up at him out of the corner of her eye.

"Plans changed," she said. "You might not want to go in there." She pointed her chin in the direction of the dorm room door.

Marc's eyebrows gained altitude significantly. He drew out a kitchen chair and sat in it.

"Pastry?" he offered lamely.

Miranda shook her head but sat up slowly. She watched as he flipped open the notebook still on the kitchen table and scanned its contents casually, with an experienced eye.

With the clarity of looking in a mirror, she now understood who

Marc was.

She watched him through hooded eyes for the signs she had felt herself all week—the careful constraint and the firm tension. With a shot of green adrenaline, a wicked smile broke on her face. "You've been lying," she said.

Marc turned to her with the first honest look she'd seen in his face, except maybe yesterday when he passed with her through mottled sunshine, when the relief of fresh air was written in his eyes.

Marc closed the notebook.

"What do you mean?" he asked, struggling to pull the screens back across his eyes.

"You're not a priest. You were never going to be one."

"Well, not exactly," he said, a moment of panic rippling across his face. "Maybe a long time ago." Found out, he relaxed into his real self. Its smoothness irritated Miranda, even while it inspired her to meet him with equal coolness and nonchalance.

"Is your name even Marc Castillo?"

"Yes, though I'm disappointed none of you recognized it," he said. "I thought you might have seen one of my books—they're usually in airports. Near the other, really more successful thrillers. Kind of near the bottom."

"Well, you can't have your cake and eat it too," she said. "Either you wanted us to recognize you or you didn't." Marc shrugged good-naturedly. "You were going to write about them," she said.

"I'm trying to break into literary fiction," he said. "I've got to start somewhere. But I don't think they're quite as interesting anymore, so I think I'll look elsewhere."

"Why?" Miranda asked, leaning forward. Though she'd been angry with him for stealing it in the first place, it irked her that he would so easily throw away their story.

"It's not as interesting when they actually get together in the end," he said. "I'll probably have to change that, and a few other things. Add some more action. Your character needs to do something drastic, like try to kill someone. Anyway, it's over now, and I missed the most important parts, so I'll probably just make it all up."

"Join the club," Miranda said, leaning back again. "That's the story of my life with Olivia." She paused, sensing an alarming camaraderie nosing its way between them. "So where are you really from?"

"New York," he said, shedding the last of his soft accent. "You're never going to trust me again, are you?" He stroked his wrist-bandage lightly with the tips of his fingers.

"Not a bit."

Miranda wondered if it would really matter to anyone if she exposed him. She wondered if it even mattered to her. She realized he was the first new friend she had made in three years. She realized he hadn't run, as Lenny had.

"But that doesn't mean we can't have lunch again today," she said at last. "I don't think my sister will make it."

"You know," Marc said, dusting his hands off over the sink and running the water briefly, "I think one of the best parts of Spain is the food."

"Really? Not the churches?" Miranda said dryly.

"Okay, you got me," he said, grinning weakly. "You going to tell me why you're okay with this?" he said, gesturing toward the dorm room.

"Sure, but you have to promise me I won't see it in print," she said. "Oh, and one more question."

"What?"

"Why pretend you're a *priest*?"

"Everyone's nice to the hip young priest. And you never have to risk vacation fling disasters," Marc said. "It was hard with the real deal around, though."

"Oh yeah? Afraid of competition?"

"No, it just cramped my style."

Marc held out his arm, with conscious affectation. Miranda rose to take it. Together, they walked out of the hostel.

11

YOU SHALL ABOVE ALL THINGS BE GLAD AND YOUNG

Miranda and Marc set out for Gothic Quarter adventure, armed with new and interesting facts about each other. She heard the bells and he smelled the lilies, and she never once stopped to worry about getting lost, except briefly when she saw someone in a shop she thought looked like Lenny's friend from yesterday, the one she was supposed to be traveling with.

When Olivia and Greg emerged timidly from their dim retreat, having finally talked about all that had happened between them, the hostel was empty and shivering, and they sat by the window to feel the warmth of the sun swarm around their bare arms. Miranda hadn't left a note. Olivia understood.

That afternoon, Olivia and Greg climbed the mountain. They left at noon and rose between the scattered trees along the road that zigzagged up, taking each turn with a gust of breath, through slanting shadows that smelled like pines, until they could look down on Barcelona through the clear air.

The castle was like a fort in a book, but Olivia didn't think of that. She saw the red vines that crawled up its massive side, blushing and blood-colored against the mud-brown stones, and the piercing sunlight on the top, where an endless Barcelona stretched around her, falling sharply to the cliffs and then the docks below, where trucks crept through thread-like driveways and containers were stacked like dingy toys. The warm wind threaded her hair as it hung loose around her shoulders, and she felt Greg's arms slip around her waist. She leaned back into him.

"Why did you leave a question mark in my room?" she asked.

He tensed, embarrassed, and tried to withdraw, but Olivia turned around to show him she was smiling.

"I just," he began, then stopped. "I read—I was reading about, um, I was reading some things about language and I thought, if you can express so much in one unspoken thing, why not put it everywhere? But I didn't have the guts to actually write it on the streets. So I just put it on a piece of paper. I thought maybe I could do that instead, write it on lots of pieces of paper and leave them everywhere, but then I was too nervous to do that, too."

Olivia laughed, but stopped when she saw his long face.

"No, no, I'm not laughing at you," she said, scooting closer to him. "It just makes so much sense."

All the little fragments of Greg she had seen throughout the week began to coalesce into a person, but there was still so much to learn. She wondered what he had been like before his mother had died. She wondered how he had taken the news.

Her face became solemn again.

"Are you still sad about your dad?" he asked.

"Yes," she said, only realizing the answer when it popped out of her mouth.

"Oh," he said. "Sorry. I thought—"

"But it's going to be okay," she said, cutting him off. "I think."

In time, they got up and moved to explore the rest of the castle.

Back at the Casa Joven, Mr. Brown listened while Hugo attempted to explain to him the music on the dance radio station. He sat and watched as a new group arrived to take Ana and Chas's beds—another pair of sisters from the States, looking very jet-lagged, unhappy, and wilted. He smiled at them, and then got up to fetch his notebook from the dormitory room. In it were the poems he thought his wife would have enjoyed.

When they had married, he was more than twenty years older than her, and had always assumed he would be the first to go. But then she got sick, and the doctors said it had been lurking in her body since before they had ever met. He never stopped copying out passages for her, though, or marking the pages he would have shown to her in their bed later in the evening.

That night, Mr. Brown and Hugo made a Thanksgiving dinner of sorts for the whole hostel: turkey sandwiches and mashed potatoes from a box. Marc invented Thanksgiving traditions like "hinkle spoons" to teach to the non-American guests. Miranda played along as if she'd known about them her whole life. Olivia was grateful to see her sister playful again.

On Friday, all the travelers went to the Cathedral. Miranda recognized Saint Sebastian, and Marc pretended to know more about him than he could really remember. Olivia and Greg stood on the roof and Mr. Brown fed the geese in the cloister. The bells tolled and the organ whistled, and Olivia never found the accordion man.

Leaving was harder. Greg's hand fell out of hers. Mr. Brown kissed her on her hair. Olivia understood that a life was unfurling in front of her, long and ribbon-like and unknown.

Miranda, watching them, found a resilience long hidden under the rotten anxiety clouding her heart.

In the end, they all went home.

Hugo and Sophie planted lilies in a box outside the window the next spring. Greg applied to college, and Mr. Brown hired an assistant pastor, a kid fresh from upstate. Marc never wrote a book about Spain. He went back to New York, where he completed his first literary novel, the story of a middle-aged writer living in New York. Miranda read it and finally gathered the courage to write him.

On an unseasonably chilly, bright September day, Olivia arrived at Cornell, and her mother drove away after leaving her with her bags stacked in a dusty, empty room. Her roommate would soon arrive and they would begin to arrange furniture and devise arbitrary and complex rules for sharing food, watching TV, and having guests.

She put her hand in the pocket of her jacket. There, her fingers ran over the well-worn edges of a letter. Greg had been the one to suggest they write to each other on paper. Now she appreciated the idea. She felt as if she was holding his hand. She told herself this was the way she could, until next time.

Outside, the trees shivered in the breezes of autumn, and loaded vans passed alongside the anxiety of a thousand freshmen hoping to feel ready for what lay ahead.

ACKNOWLEDGMENTS

I owe too many people too large a debt of gratitude to squeeze onto one little page. Here's the abridged version.

To my mom, novelist Libby Malin Sternberg, for being my best writing teacher, for editing early versions of this story, and for supporting me, as a tireless counselor, through subsequent revisions.

To Dad, for being my biggest fan, and my brothers for telling me I'm nuts for everything I do except writing novels.

To Bruce Bortz, my publisher, for giving me a chance and for holding my hand through the phone. To Harrison Demchick, my editor, for helping me take a sock-drawer manuscript and turn it into something I can confidently wear in public.

To Vanessa, my one-time roommate, who filled me in on what to do when your character refuses to talk or eat.

And to all the friends I traveled with, wrote with, and experienced with.

ABOUT THE AUTHOR

Hannah Sternberg lives and works in Washington, D.C. In 2009, she graduated from Johns Hopkins University in Baltimore, Maryland with a major in Film and Media Studies and a minor in Writing Seminars, feeling like the most unemployable girl in the world. She now works for the Washington D.C.-based Heritage Foundation.

In addition to writing, she spends her spare time making short independent films and freaking out about hypothetical travel accidents.

To learn more about Hannah, her creative work, and her pet bamboo, visit her at www.hannahsternberg.com.

3/12